Someone's Daughter

SOMEONE'S DAUGHTER

WILL TO SURVIVE

*Ramy —
Here's one for your shelf — or to give away. I don't give a frog :)
Thanks for all your encouragement,
Rhys*

RHYS SHAW

Someone's Daughter © 2022 Rhys Shaw

First Edition © 2022

Someone's Daughter is a work of fiction. Names, characters, places, and incidents are the product of the author's imagination or are used fictitiously. Any resemblance to actual persons, living or dead, events or locales is entirely coincidental.

Rhys Shaw

www.rhysshawauthor@gmail.com

All rights reserved. No part of this publication may be reproduced, distributed or transmitted in any form or by any means, including photocopying, recording, or other electronic or mechanical methods, without the prior written permission of the author, except in the case of brief quotations embodied in critical reviews and certain other noncommercial uses permitted by copyright law.

ISBN paperback. 979-8-9861718-0-7
Publisher: Patient Hawk Publishing

Please note this novel depicts issues of emotional, sexual, and physical abuse, sexual violence, and death. Content which some readers may find triggering. The descriptions are graphic, but important to the reality of how women were treated in the 14th Century and are still treated in many parts of the world, today. This story is entirely fictional, set in a fictional land.

PROLOGUE

Our daughters shall carry the earth. They will mend her, replenish her with children, heal her with wisdom.

Our daughters shall raise their sons in the ways of the land and people, to bring about peace and clarity for what must happen.

Our daughters will right the wrongs of men who knew no better, and of men who knew the truth, but did not care.

I

Alaria was trapped. Inside her dream, she felt someone was hovering above her, staring down, ready to pounce. They grabbed her wrists, and she flailed about, trying to protect herself. Her eyes opened. It was not a dream. She was being held down by a tall man with piercing blue eyes. He was laughing as he tightened his grip on her.

"Let me go! How dare you even be in my bed chamber." She struggled, trying to kick her legs, but with his firm grip and her heavy bedclothes, it was a lost cause.

The man only leered at her as other guards entered her room. She heard one of them ask where the other two royal bitches were. Pulling her to a standing position, the blue-eyed man told her to get dressed, or not. He said it didn't matter to him. As soon as he released her, she grabbed her thick dressing gown, pulling it around herself to stop his eyes from boring into her, and put on some socks for warmth. Morning had not yet broken, and her fires hadn't been lit. It was bitter and cold within her room.

Her breath looked like smoke in the frigid air as she asked, "Why are you here, and what is the meaning of this?"

Before anyone answered, the younger princesses were dragged into her room and shoved towards her, both crying and terrified.

Alaria ran to them and tried to calm them down. "Shhh, hush now, it will all be alright."

Neither of them had on more than their sleeping dresses, so she gathered up a blanket for the youngest, Genison, and another dressing gown for Soria. Both of the young girls stepped behind their older sister for protection, and she repeated her questions, trying to muster up as much authority as a thirteen-year-old could find.

A pathway was cleared as Traintor, the Earl of Newark, came striding into her room in that awkward and ungainly way that portly chaps stride. "Good morning, princesses. Follow all orders, and no harm will come to you. Let my men escort you to your new living chambers. No need to worry, your parents will be joining you soon. I only wanted to round you up first, as my collateral, just in case your father or any of his men tried to stop us. As of today, I am the new ruler of Welexia."

The princesses were speechless and frozen in disbelief, but they jumped when he shouted, spewing spittle everywhere, "Well, did you not hear me? Bow down, you ungrateful wenches. I am your king!"

Alaria took each of her sisters' hands, and they all bowed to this abysmal man. Genison and Soria were both still crying.

Newark seemed offended by this and spoke directly to Alaria. "I advise you to get your sisters under control. I can always send them with Creavy, here. He has ways of training young girls."

At the mention of his name, Creavy, the blue-eyed man, stepped forward and spoke. "Yes, your majesty, I would love to take these young ladies off of your 'ands. I do 'ave ways of getting them to obey me." He was ogling all three of them but seemed particularly focused on Alaria and smacked his lips, making offensive noises as he stared at her.

She met his gaze with hatred, which only seemed to excite him. Not wishing to end up with him, she turned her attention to Newark before bowing again and speaking. "Your Majesty, may my sisters and I gather some warm clothing, please, before we are escorted to our new chambers?"

Newark snorted and waved an acknowledgement of sorts.

She took immediate action and began stuffing warm socks, slippers, and wraps into a large bag. Then she bowed again and said, "Thank you, King Traintor." The words felt like razors in her throat, but she knew she could play this game if it meant their lives were now dependent upon this wretched man.

Newark scratched his crotch and said to Creavy, "Well, perhaps they will end up with you soon, but for now, I will unite them with their parents. I am not evil, after all." Newark, Creavy, and all of the guards laughed at this. Alaria, Soria, and Genison were stone-faced.

They were led down the hallway. This wasn't right, thought Alaria. Where were all the servants? Why had no one sounded the alarm about what was happening? The doorway to her mother's lady maid's room was open, and she saw poor Brigit laid out on the cold stone floor. An enormous bruise covered her face, and it was unclear whether she was alive or dead. Stepping between her sisters and the doorway to block their view, she hurried them along.

It was no use, she may have shielded them from seeing Brigit, but the hallway was a bloodbath of dead soldiers and servants who had been going about their morning, readying everything for the royal family, when they were surprised. Trays were spilled, logs being carried to light fires were scattered, soldiers who clearly put up a fight lay dead. Their faces showing the disbelief and fear of their last dying thoughts. Blood was everywhere, and trying to avoid stepping in it proved difficult.

Soria was gasping to breathe as her tears overcame her, and she gulped for air. Fearing the threat from Newark about sending one or all of them with Creavy, Alaria turned to Soria and pulled her sister's face into her shoulder while still holding Genison's hand. She herself was terrified and could only imagine what her younger sisters were feeling. She must remain strong. There would be time for her own tears later.

At last, they arrived at a part of the castle where the young ladies had never been. It was much darker and dingier here, and a few rats scurried down the hallway, running towards them and passing them as if trying to escape from this hellhole. A large door with iron bars creaked open, and the girls were shoved inside. There was a clanging of metal as the door was locked with a padlock the size of a hand. It smelled like rotting piles of food before they were buried or eaten by the castle pigs.

Genison vomited. Soria wailed. Alaria pulled her clothing up to cover her nose and mouth and looked around, taking in their surroundings. Surely the new, self-appointed king did not realize where they had been taken. A mistake must have been made. She hurried to the door to ask a guard, but he only laughed at her and spat on the floor.

"No mistake, missy. Welcome to your new abode."

2

Hearing a commotion outside of his bedchamber, the king sat up. The sun had only just begun to crest the horizon, spilling a hazy orange light into the royal chambers. He looked over at his wife, sound asleep, and waited for the noises to pass. The footsteps and the frenzy were getting louder, closer. He reached over to wake her just as men entered their room, shouting at him to get to his feet.

In his confusion, he stumbled from his bed to demand who was responsible for this intrusion upon his sacred space when, from the doorway, several large men wearing an unknown crest cleared a path, and the Earl of Newark entered with a smirk upon his round face. "Ah, glad we didn't have to awaken you from your slumber, old man. Although, I can see that your wife certainly needs her beauty sleep. Seize them," he barked, and the men came forward to grab him.

The queen cried out in fear and confusion as she was dragged from their bed. He felt helpless. All of the rumors he had been hearing about the Earl of Newark were true. He didn't want to believe them, and yet here he was, taking control of Welexia and the Crown.

The king and queen, with a soldier on either side of them gripping their arms, were escorted to the dungeon and thrown into a dark damp cell. The king saw his innocent daughters hiding in the corner, terrified of what was happening to them. His anger at seeing them there was replaced with relief that their lives had been spared. He surmised they were only kept alive because they were female and not heirs to the throne as a son would've been. The younger princesses were in complete shock, not understanding why anyone would treat their family in such a cruel manner. They whimpered and cowered like frightened puppies, and their parents did their best to console them. Only the eldest, Alaria, sat upright, telling her sisters to try to be brave. When her gaze met her father's, he knew she understood the dangerous situation they were in.

"Do not worry, everything will be fine," he said. He knew he was giving them false hope because, if the Earl had already turned the king's own men, they did not stand a chance. For the right price, it would've been easy to turn many of his protectors, yet he knew in his heart it would've been impossible to turn his noble Bracknor. He would either be in another dungeon cell, holed up somewhere in hiding, or dead from fighting for his king. Not wanting to believe his last thought, he put all his energy into hoping Bracknor was indeed in hiding and organizing a siege of the castle to rescue them and help him restore order. With this thought, he looked at his terrified, disheveled family, knowing he must remain strong for them. Somewhere beyond the cell wall, a cock crowed.

3

It was Bracknor's responsibility to keep the king safe and informed, and he took his duties seriously. They'd known each other since they were lads, their pecking order Oshinor at the top, Bracknor right beside him as a friend and protector. It had been this way since their youth and the first time they were attacked by young scoundrels when playing and swimming in the forest. Bracknor was the last one to come out of the swimming hole when he heard malicious laughter. He crept towards the ruckus, careful not to crack any twigs and alert them. Peering through the brambles, he counted three lads unknown to him, shoving Oshinor around between them. They were all participating, but one boy was the ringleader. He was the one to be taken down. Picking up a rough stone, Bracknor flung it with an archer's precision straight into the head of the leader, striking him on the temple. Blood spurted out, and the boy jumped in surprise. He staggered and would've fallen over if one of his mates had not held him up. Before they could recover, a roaring Bracknor came bursting through the brambles, causing scratches oozing with fresh blood to cover his still-glistening naked skin. He was a sight indeed, and the bullies turned tail and ran, screaming as they did so. He helped Oshinor up from where he had been knocked down, and they rolled around with laughter.

"Look at you! You look like a crazed beast!" said Oshinor, tossing Bracknor his clothing.

Bracknor looked down at his bloody, sweaty body and put his breeches on. "Well, better a crazed, naked beast than you getting a good hiding!" he chided.

"So true. Thank you."

That was one of many times when Bracknor used his brawn and bravery to rescue Oshinor. To now flee the castle when an informant told him King Oshinor and his family were to be taken just before dawn and locked up in the dungeon tore at his conscience. His friendship wanted him to stay and fight to the death, but his military training told him he was outnumbered.

For several months, the people had seemed restless, and he suspected some of his men were turning their loyalty over to the Earl of Newark. All of a sudden, they were flush with funds, whoring and drinking more than usual. They were also getting rather friendly with Hildebrand, one of the king's accountants. Bracknor had never trusted Hildebrand, but Oshinor always wanted to find the good in people and insisted he was a loyal accountant. Loyal only to himself was more like it, in Bracknor's opinion. The name Hildebrand had indeed come up from the informant, and it was no surprise. He had been a part of the brothel in the castle for years, yet when confronted by King Oshinor, he explained that the women down below were only training as servants for both the castle kitchens and the wealthier people of the kingdom. Naively, King Oshinor believed him. Hildebrand assured the king he knew of no brothel. The king wanted all that was best for his kingdom, but his trustworthy nature and naivety were his downfall.

Bracknor knew Lord Newark's men would kill him as soon as look at him. The only way to save the king and his family would be to flee now, form an allegiance, and return. It may take years, but he was determined to do so. His heart broke as he rode his horse away from the castle under the cover of darkness. He prayed Oshinor knew he had not betrayed him and that he would return one day to rescue his friend, as he had always done.

4

King Oshinor had always been a man of the people, really caring for them. Sitting on the throne from a very young age, it took him several years before he felt confident enough to rule as he truly wished. Once he felt empowered enough, he gradually forced wealthy landowners to pay a larger tax than they were used to, to be fairer to their workers - allowing them two days off a week - and to charge less rent for those living on their lands. He believed that, in doing so, their workers would respect them, thrive as a community, and actually get more work done. He was correct. For a while, things were better. People felt pride in themselves, as they were able to take better care of their families. They found joy in life.

Those with enslaved people had to free them. They could keep them on as workers, but only if they paid them a decent wage and only if the now free people wished to remain. Some were hired by their previous owners. Others went their own way to choose what they wanted to do and where they wished to live. Many resented the king for this. As far as they were concerned, they had already paid for these humans, their property, so why should they continue to pay? It was rumored some were living in the same horrendous conditions they had always lived in and threatened with their lives or the lives of their loved ones if they told anyone or complained about their situation.

Perhaps the peasants were naive, but they were hopeful things would continue to improve and began having dreams of an even better life. They educated their children, something never done before. Teachers came from far away and organized makeshift schools for anyone who wanted to learn. Food and shelter were provided by the villagers, and they survived on this kindness. Seeing others learn and knowing they played a part in this was extra payment. It was a utopia of sorts, people caring for each other in ways they hadn't done in many years. Overall, the changes the king made had been a good thing: releasing the slaves, empowering the workers, placing a sense of value on everyone's life, not just the wealthy.

How could anyone know that underneath this prosperous and idyllic facade lurked a darker force? The lords and ladies of the court and the wealthy landowners were not happy with King Oshinor's revival of the everyday man and wanted things to be the way they were before, and even stricter for the peasants. They devised a plan to oust King Oshinor, by whatever means necessary, and replace him with their chosen one, the Earl of Newark, the future King Traintor. They met quietly at first, so as not to tip off the king, slowly building up their forces and supporters. It seemed almost everyone who had thrived in the former economy wanted things to go back to the old ways. They weren't making enough money off their own land and workers now, and if things continued, there wouldn't be a proper divide between the classes. This was absurd and could not happen.

Their followers grew, and they would go amongst the people and cause carefully planned arguments and fights to break out, wanting to divide the peasants as much as possible. The teachers had come from far away, and no one knew much about them, so it was easy to slander their names and talk about their horrific pasts. Once the seed was planted and a teacher stopped receiving food and shelter, they had no choice but to move on. School, once again, became something only for those who could afford to pay for it.

They infiltrated the local taverns and started brawls amongst friends and neighbors, saying they had stolen from each other, and planting items in places that convinced the people there were indeed many thieves amongst their neighbors and former friends.

They withheld some of their crops from them, claiming the workers had not worked hard enough and therefore they'd had a bad harvest. The workers knew this was not the case, and some began to pilfer food, even though being caught would've ended in hanging or the stocks. Others were going hungry and resenting those who had been stealing, blaming them for the shortages of food.

The peaceful people became suspicious of others, and the community was no longer coming together unless it was to complain about someone or something. Friends turned against one another, family members turned against one another. An ugly hatred arose, surrounding the former slaves, causing a division of people based on their skin color or wealth.

The instigators were pleased and presented their chosen one as a savior to the people in the wintertime when many were starving. He alone would restore order, send the outcasts away that were causing all the problems, once again unite families with their neighbors—neighbors who were like them—make more money for the people, somehow find them food to eat, and make things better off. He wouldn't say how he would do these things, but because he was an earl, he obviously knew how to take care of business and they should trust him. He also had money at his disposal, so they needn't worry about the details but should just leave it to him.

According to Lord Newark, things hadn't been going well under King Oshinor, and he only wanted to make them better. He cited examples of events that had been secretly organized by his dark army. He said treasonous things about King Oshinor, and no one stopped him. The people could not believe how unafraid he seemed when slandering their king. Many thought Newark brave and intelligent, a wise man when it came to business matters, and agreed with him that since the slaves had been freed, they had taken some of their jobs, jobs that should've gone to their sons and daughters. Yes, they needed a strong brave leader to make their lives better, and this was the man to do it.

Some could not believe what they were observing. How could people believe the lies the earl was spewing? He spoke like a crazed man, and he spoke of uniting them, but a division was taking place before their very eyes. They tried sharing their thoughts with their neighbors but were met with laughter and sometimes anger. Those who believed in the earl didn't understand why anyone wouldn't trust him. He was a man saying the things they had wanted to say all these years. He wasn't afraid of anyone or anything. They needed someone like this to be their king, and if you disagreed, then you must be insane or some kind of traitor.

Blythe, a farmer, and his wife, Waleda, were amongst those who thought madness had taken over their village and kingdom. They failed to see any decent qualities in Lord Newark but soon realized they were in the minority. They suspected others felt like they did but were afraid to talk openly about it because there were spies, and they had witnessed the sudden disappearance of friends, being told they had left for better lives elsewhere. Never mind that these friends had left their homes without taking any of their belongings. No one was supposed to notice this. It concerned them, and they chose to only speak about it in the safety of their own home.

Their two children, Mildrea and Farnsly, listened carefully to what their parents had to say. Farnsly was walking the valley between boyhood and manhood and, truth be told, found it all a bit frightening. Mildrea had lived a few more winters than her brother, and she wondered if her parents were out of touch. All her friends thought Lord Newark was incredible, so she believed it too. Knowing her parents' thoughts, she didn't voice her own to them.

Suddenly, news spread that King Oshinor had stepped down. Ill health was cited as the reason. There was shock and confusion. No king had ever voluntarily stepped down before. Perhaps even King Oshinor knew the earl was a better option for running their kingdom? Once Oshinor was gone, no time was wasted in replacing him with Lord Newark. A pompous ceremony took place, and King Traintor was now the official king of Welexia.

The rumor was spread that Oshinor and his family had fled the kingdom, embarrassed at what a failure they had been to their people. Many chose to believe these rumors. If only they had known that King Oshinor, his wife, and their daughters were being held prisoner in his own castle by the earl, they may have felt differently—some of them, at least.

It was all a bit surreal. People no longer trusted their neighbors and friends. Spies lived amongst them, and if you were reported to King Traintor as a traitor, you would suddenly disappear. Former slaves were arrested and forced back into slavery. Many chose to take their own lives instead. Workers had their two days off taken away. A few hours on the sabbath were all you needed to attend church, but you could go back to work after you had cleansed your soul. Although workdays were more now, wages did not go up. Some landowners even charged more money for their workers to lease the cottages on their land. Pay or move out. People from other villages, who had dreams of integrating into King Traintor's new kingdom, would happily replace you if this was the case.

Waleda, Blythe, and their son Farnsly continued to work the land but found it difficult finding enough food since King Traintor had taken over. Mildrea, their daughter, left the following spring, when the snow had melted and the trees were in bloom, stating her parents were simple peasants, foolish to believe their lives would ever mean anything. She heard they were hiring young women in the castle kitchens and was determined to find a better life. Her departure was ugly. Waleda begged her to stay, but she held fast.

Eventually, Blythe conceded she may in fact have a better life working in the kitchens of the castle than she could ever have working with them, so the family wished her well and asked her to keep in touch.

5

Mildrea hitched a ride on the back of a milk wagon and eventually found herself just outside the castle walls. She was bustled into the crowd of shoppers and street urchins darting in and out of the jostling shoppers. There were merchants set up with wares she didn't recognize. Colors and patterns of cloth she never knew existed and reflective glassware of many colors, showing rainbows without any rain. She was fascinated. All of the crockery in her life had been made of clay or wood.

There were divine pungent smells of spices, perfumes, and roasting meats, and the merchants taunted the shoppers by calling out to them, "Come, sample my succulent meat," and "Feel the texture of this cloth, you have never touched anything so sublime."

They weren't really talking to Mildrea, as she was

in her peasant dress made of rough wool. She was clean and beautiful, in her natural and innocent way, but she clearly had no money. She felt almost as if in a dream, until she rounded a corner and heard flies buzzing and was taken aback by the putrid smell of feces, urine, and the rotting flesh of traitors to the king who had been hanged and left for all to see as an example. She gasped when she realized one of the men hanging had been a friend of her family's. He was like an uncle to her and always such a kind man. One of his eyeballs was hanging out of the socket and resting on his cheek. As she stared in disbelief, a bird came along and plucked the hanging orb and flew away with the treasure.

With tears streaming down her face, she grasped her shawl to her mouth and nose to hide the smell and ran back into the more fragrant part of the market. Stunned, she sat down on a rock near the castle gate and was thinking about her parents and hoping they would be alright. It wasn't long before a throng of people were all around her, and she stood to see what was going on. There was a loud thunk of metal striking metal, followed by a creaking noise and then the crowd sank into a reverent hush. Once the huge castle gate opened, royal horsemen rode out, followed by the king himself who was being carried in a palanquin. Although he was surrounded by his men, Mildrea caught a glimpse of him through the curtains.

Everyone bowed or curtsied in silence, then abruptly people were chanting, "King Traintor, King Traintor, long live King Traintor!"

Caught up in the excitement, Mildrea forgot all about the rotting men she had recently stumbled upon. This was definitely where she wanted to be, not on a farm working hard until she died. She was young, and the castle, the king, and his followers were exciting. She decided that, from this moment forth, she would do whatever it took to change her life and leave that peasant girl behind her. Being youthful, fresh-faced, and beautiful meant it didn't take long to be noticed. Being clean was an added bonus, and the man who was now beside Mildrea startled her when he first spoke. So caught up in the frenzy of seeing the king, she hadn't realized she was flanked by two men, one tall with intense blue eyes, the other shorter with a scruffy beard.

"Well 'ello, missy, I don't believe we've seen you round 'ere before," said the blue-eyed man.

"Naw, I don't believe we 'ave," said his friend. "I never forget a pretty face." He crinkled up his face when he smiled, and Mildrea noticed some crumbs lodged in his beard.

The blue-eyed man spoke again. "Are you lost? Would you like my friend and I to assist you in finding your way?"

Her stomach had a knot in it, and she tried to sound confident when she answered, "Oh, I'm not lost. I've just moved here from… far away. I heard I could find work in the castle."

The men shared a knowing look, and the man with the blue eyes said, "Well, it's your lucky day. Let me introduce myself. I'm Creavy and me mate 'ere is Jonesy. We just so 'appen to work for the king, 'elping him find employees and such. Now, if you'll just follow me, we can take you straight to the person to get you all set up." He bowed and nodded his head.

Mildrea wasn't sure if she should run away or indeed follow Creavy. He was walking straight towards the open castle gate, and she thought he really must be someone important if he could so easily walk into the castle. Besides, Jonesy was walking so close behind her, she could feel his hot breath on her neck, and she wasn't sure she could get away from him if he didn't want her to.

As they arrived at the open gate, Creavy nodded to the guards, and they nodded back. Mildrea couldn't believe they were now inside the castle wall, and all of her fears disappeared as Creavy turned around and winked at her. Perhaps he did know how to help her find a job. She reminded herself that she wanted to change her life, and things seemed to be going well. There were so many people, and it seemed like an extension of the nicer stalls outside. Small corrals with goats, pigs, and chickens were interspersed with clotheslines filled with fresh laundry, gently blowing in the breeze. She was grateful there were no hanging bodies inside here. Children were running, playing, and laughing. Women were stirring large cauldrons of delicious-smelling stews, and Mildrea's stomach started rumbling. It had been a long two days of travel, and all she'd eaten since her porridge and bread when she left her parents' home was some dried bread and fruit. Jonesy was clearly hungry too, and he headed toward a cauldron. The woman stirring it scooped stew into a bowl for him. He growled as he grabbed her arse, and the woman slapped him on the cheek. Then he tossed a coin in the air, and she caught it, with a wink herself. Slurping the stew down in one gulp, he burped and then tossed the bowl on the ground towards her.

"You filthy bastard," the woman said, laughing.

Wiping his beard and mouth on his sleeve, he returned to Creavy and Mildrea. They stopped near a door, and Creavy told Mildrea to wait there with Jonesy, saying he would be right back. She felt safe enough, surrounded by so many people in the castle yard, and when Jonesy walked over to sit in the shade, she joined him. After a few minutes, the door opened and Creavy came out, motioning for her to follow him inside. Butterflies fluttered in her stomach as she walked towards the open castle door. It was a plain door on the bottom, but it might lead straight to the kitchens and her future. She was nervous but told herself the heavy feeling in the pit of her stomach was just excitement about her new life.

It was very dark inside the underbelly of the castle. The ceiling was low, and the torches in the hallways were spread quite thin. It was dingier than Mildrea had imagined it would be. After growing up with low ceilings, she had fantasized about beautiful high-ceilinged kitchens in the castle, where fragrant herbs would be hung on racks that had to be lowered down with a rope. Not to worry, she told herself, this might just be the pathway. Creavy stopped outside of a door, knocked a few times, and then waited for an answer.

"Come in," said a woman's voice.

Mildrea felt relief at hearing a woman's voice and nervously smiled at Creavy, who winked at her in reply. He pushed open the door and allowed her to enter, then closed the door behind her without following. The sickly sweet smell is what hit her first, yet she couldn't quite make it out. She had smelled older people when they didn't properly look after themselves and thought this might be that, but the woman was masking it somehow with some sort of sweet, almost overpowering smell.

It wasn't a pleasant smell, but she didn't want to be rude, and hoping to make a good first impression, she curtsied and said, "Hello."

A small, rather frail-looking woman stepped out of the shadows towards her. Saying nothing, she turned her head, almost birdlike, as she inspected Mildrea from top to bottom. Then walking all the way around her, the woman grabbed Mildrea's arse, startling the lass. "A farm girl, eh? Not too much meat on the bones. Well, we can fix that up with a few good meals. Still, not bad, not bad at all."

Mildrea felt this was a good time to speak. "Yes, ma'am, I do come from a farm, and I'm a good worker. I'm a good cook too and a fast learner, so I'm really hoping you can find a place for me in one of the kitchens here at the castle. I will wash dishes, clean the floors, whatever needs doing. Like I said, I'm a good worker."

The woman's pinched, wrinkled face looked straight at Mildrea, showing no emotion, and then she burst out laughing. "Yes, you will be a fast learner, alright, I'll make sure of that." Then she shuffled back across the room, sat in her chair, and continued looking at Mildrea, smiling at her.

Mildrea stood there, feeling awkward in the silence, until Creavy came in and motioned for her to follow him to another room. Again, he held the door open for her, but this time, he followed her into the room and bolted the door behind them. There was only a bed in this room, and when she opened her mouth to speak, he struck her hard across the cheek. She put her hand to her stinging cheek, frightened and not understanding what was going on, as Creavy reached up and ripped her dress off her shoulders and down to her waist.

He stood there staring at her breasts with his icy blue eyes, licking his lips, and then sighed. "Too bad I can't properly sample the wares meself. Too bad. Not yet anyway. You is a virgin, and men will pay good money for that. Once you're broken in, I'll 'ave you, you pretty little princess. What did you say your name was?"

Terrified and shaking, Mildrea looked back at him with tears in her eyes. She was not going to tell this man her name. Not now. Not ever. If he spoke her name, it would be poisoned, so she wouldn't share it.

"Cat got your tongue? That's alright. I don't need you to talk. I can't 'ave you yet, but I can 'ave a sample taste before anyone else gets to. That's the deal me and the madam 'ave worked out, you see. Just a taste, but that's enough for me, for now anyway. You see, madam trusts me to taste and then stop meself. Jonesy can't stop 'imself, that's why 'e no longer gets to sample the goods."

He grabbed her by the hair, threw her down on the bed, and tied her hands above her head to a leather strap hanging from the headboard. Then he lifted her skirt and smiled at her as he licked his lips, lowered himself, and buried his nose and mouth into her. She cried out in anger and then stopped herself. She wasn't going to give this man any emotion either. She just lay there as Creavy did what he said he would do, he sampled her flavor. Then he stopped and released his erection from his trousers. She wondered if this would be the time he couldn't stop, but he simply relieved himself and came all over her clothes and breasts.

Then he smoothed her skirt back down, leaned close as if to kiss her, nearly touched his lips to hers, and breathed her own smell back into her mouth as he said, "Yeah, that'll do nicely, my princess. Very nicely, indeed. Glad to be of service in finding you employment. You 'ave a lovely day now, miss." Then he bit her nipple, licked some of his juices off her chest, stood up, and left.

She heard the door bolt behind him and lay there motionless with tears stinging her eyes and cheeks. She had no idea how much time had passed when the door opened and the madam and Creavy entered the room again. The madam came over to the bed, sat down next to her, and then whilst keeping eye contact with Mildrea, reached under her skirt and inserted a rough finger into her. Mildrea was determined not to cry out, but she couldn't stop the tears running down her cheeks.

"Well done, Creavy. I don't know how you control yourself, but you always manage it. Well done. Once she's been deflowered, you'll be nicely compensated. Untie her hands, then you can visit one of the other girls if you still need some attention. Of course, there's always me if you're feeling really frisky." Madam threw her head back and laughed at herself. Creavy was laughing too as he released her hands from their bondage. Then the old crone shuffled out of the room with Creavy following behind.

As soon as they'd gone, Mildrea gathered her torn dress up around her breasts and sat up in the bed in a sickly sweet-smelling fog that Madam had left behind and fears of the unknown. She looked around at the dingy, filthy room, stunned. She crawled from the bed and went to the chipped basin of water nearby. Using a piece of her torn dress, she began scrubbing her breasts. The water was freezing cold, but she was determined to remove Creavy's seed and scrubbed herself until her skin was raw. Unable to fix her dress, she wrapped her shawl around her and sat in the corner of the room on the dusty floor. She must be having a nightmare, as it was too horrible to be true.

6

Waleda was stirring their stew, which was mostly broth, over the fire one afternoon when she heard a commotion outside. She went to the doorway and saw her husband and other villagers being chased down by men on horses, who would whip and knock them down whenever they caught them. Confused by what was happening, she ran outside and saw her son also being attacked. He tripped and fell flat onto his face as a horse and rider reared up then came down, with the horse's foot landing on his back. Waleda screamed as she heard a bone-cracking sound. Her son cried out and then fell silent. The horsemen rode away as she ran to her son. Her husband staggered over, and they sobbed over the broken, dead body of their son, Farnsly.

Their friend Gyles, who had been knocked down, pulled himself up from the ground and came over to help Waleda get Blythe into their cottage and onto the bed. "Anyone who has ever spoken against the king is being targeted. My former neighbor is now housed in the castle. He must be giving names to the king's men of anyone disloyal to Newark. Seems they are being taken out one by one, or field by field, as today seems to suggest. You escaped with your life today, Blythe, but you and Waleda need to get away tonight," Gyles said.

"But what about our son? We need to bury him. We can't just leave," said Waleda.

"I'll bury your son. I've never spoken out against the king to anyone but you two. I've been careful. I'll be alright."

Blythe put his hand on Waleda's arm and said, "He's right, my love, we need to leave tonight."

"So be it," she said. "But first, I will say goodbye to my son."

She and Gyles walked outside to where the crumpled body of Farnsly lay in the field. Brushing his hair back from his young face, she kissed his forehead and said a silent prayer, thanking the goddesses that his death was swift, at least. Rising from her knees, she thanked Gyles and handed him the blanket she had been carrying. The field was littered with broken bodies. All around, people were tending to their wounded or dead. Gyles assured her that Farnsly would be taken care of, sure and proper. He said he would make a false grave for Blythe also, as the king's men were sure to return.

Waleda knew there wasn't much time, but she insisted on wrapping her husband's broken ribs and tending to his wounds before they did anything else. As he lay on the bed in their cottage, she grabbed anything she thought might be useful for their life on the run. Pots, bowls, animal skins, knives, a hammer, blankets, and any food they had all went into baskets. She was careful to make it look as though someone was still living there because she didn't want anyone coming after them until they had a few days' head start. Once everything was packed up, she looked around their home, not knowing if they would ever return. It was now the middle of the night and seemed a perfect time for slipping away.

Waleda took a deep breath and helped Blythe to his feet and out the door. "Come, my love, we must be going now. Let us not dwell on what has been but face whatever is to come together." She did her best to conceal her heartbreak, but Blythe heard it in the crackle of her voice.

Leaving Farnsly to be buried by someone else tore at her heart, but she knew that to keep Blythe alive, it was the only way. Taking one of the plowhorses, she insisted Blythe ride upon her, as he was wounded. They walked all through the night and stopped when the sun rose. Laying out a blanket on a bed of leaves, they crawled under low tree branches to get some much-needed sleep.

After a few hours, Waleda woke up and looked at her bruised husband. He was asleep still, but he was restless, so she quietly crawled out from under their makeshift tree shelter. She took the horse and went in search of water, letting the old mare lead her through the woods, figuring she would find it easier. The mare didn't let her down, and she filled a leather bag with water for the horse and some skins for Blythe and herself. There were fish flitting about in the stream, and the thought of fresh fish for breakfast was enticing. Not wanting Blythe to worry, she decided she'd best head back. She planned on returning without the mare later to try her hand at fishing, something she hadn't done since childhood.

Walking back to where Blythe was sleeping, she wondered where they would go. They were essentially enemies of the king and couldn't go anywhere near the castle. They would have to go to another village and take on new identities to begin again. The thought of starting anew, at their age, was terrifying. Blythe was older than her and had outlived many of their neighbors. How would these two silver-haired people convince strangers they were simply travelers and not on the run from the king?

Blythe was awake and sitting up when she returned. They ate bread Waleda had baked only yesterday, which seemed ages ago. She began gathering sticks for a small fire to cook one of the birds she had grabbed from their house. Blythe thought they shouldn't spend too much time making camp until they had more distance between them and the castle. She couldn't understand why the king would send anyone looking for them. Besides, several men and their son had been killed yesterday. How would they know they hadn't killed Blythe amongst them? Her husband had a strong will, but hers was stronger, and finally she put her foot down.

"I am building a fire, we are eating one of those birds, and you will rest. Now that is that."

He knew better than to argue with her any more about it.

Returning to the stream to clean their dishes and taking bits of bird innards to entice the fish with, she succeeded in catching three medium-sized fish for their supper later in the day. One for her, one for Blythe, and one for the mare, whom she named Kindness. Blythe laughed when she told him her name, but she explained the mare had carried him all night, led her to water this morning, and had been most accommodating even though they had taken her away from her home.

"She would've crossed those fields one hundred times today already. She's having a holiday compared to that," he said.

Smiling, she replied, "Even so, Kindness is what she is."

Waleda changed Blythe's bandages on his wounds and hoped the ribs were wrapped tightly enough to heal, then they lay down to sleep some more, planning to head out once darkness came. She fell into a very disturbed sleep, filled with visions of her son being chased to his death.

Blythe put his hand over her mouth, stirring her awake. There was someone nearby, and the mare whinnied softly. Kindness was tied about three rods away so they could see her, but hopefully anyone finding her wouldn't immediately find them. Waleda reached for the knife strapped to her waist and crawled out from under the branches. Blythe tried to grab her wrist to stop her, but she gave him a determined look, and he understood she needed to be prepared for anything. Although he may not be able to fight much, she handed him another knife, just in case it came to it.

Peering through the leaves, she could see a man on horseback. His horse was standing near Kindness, and the two of them were snorting together. The shadows were long, and the dusk made it difficult to see. Her vision had gotten a little blurry as she aged, and sometimes small details were difficult to see, but she could see that he wasn't dressed in royal clothing and decided she'd better make her presence known or risk losing their mare. "Evening," she said walking out into the open.

Her tactic of surprise had worked, and he flinched a little as he took in the woman emerging from the woods. His eyes landed on her hand clenching her knife, and she turned the blade just a little to let him know she was prepared for whatever trouble he might bring.

Motioning with her head, she said, "There's water down that way, and you can catch yourself some fish for you and your horse. My husband and I don't want any trouble, and surely these woods are large enough for all of us."

He crinkled up his face into a disingenuous smile, revealing icy blue eyes beneath his craggy brow. "Nah, I don't want no trouble either. I'll just be on me way, as you seem to 'ave this plot of land squatted already. Evening, madam." He nodded his head and rode away slowly.

When he had gone a decent distance, Waleda approached the mare and buried her face into the horse's mane, letting out the breath she had been holding and easing up her grip on the knife. Kindness whinnied, and Waleda sighed as hot tears of relief streamed down her cheeks. Although frightened, not having seen her daughter in over two winters and seeing her husband beaten and their son murdered only yesterday meant she was not a woman to mess with this evening. She was soon to discover a new inner strength, and crossing her might prove dangerous, even fatal, to anyone who did so.

Blythe was up and hiding behind a tree when she returned to their campsite. He had his knife at the ready yet was most relieved when she told him the stranger had gone on his way. "Don't ever do that again, Waleda. I was so worried about you."

"Ha, it was him you should've been worried about. I was the one with the big knife."

They packed up their camp, with Blythe doing as much as he could. He was in a lot of pain but wanted to help. He even said he would walk tonight and Waleda should ride. She gave him one of her looks that said she would not budge, and eventually he agreed to get onto Kindness's back. After helping him onto the horse, they set off for another night on their new life journey.

Walking through the woods at night set Waleda's mind to playing tricks on her. She saw shadows cast from the moon and was sure they were dragons and ghosts, only to discover dead trees and reflections in puddles. The breeze in the leaves played a song that was at once beautifully mesmerizing and terrifyingly unknown. When she heard a blood-curdling scream in the distance, she told herself it was most likely just a bird. But other than owls, birds shouldn't be awake at night. Shaking the fear from her mind, she convinced herself it was just an owl and its prey crying out as it was caught.

7

Mildrea barely remembered what it had been like living with her parents and her brother. She always thought that living on a farm and doing the same thing day in and day out, without any chance of a change, was boring. She would've married one of the other young lads and settled into her own cottage on the estate. She would've cooked for him and their children who would surely come, go and visit her mother during the day and exchange ideas on how to prepare dishes, to change things up a bit, yet it would mostly be the same thing every day.

Now, she was living a life she had never ever imagined she would be living. It was also pretty much the same thing day in and day out, yet she would give anything to be back with her family on their farm.

Her day began by getting up, cleaning up her sparse room of whatever bottles, lost clothing, or trinkets may have been left behind. She would shake out her bedding, changing the linens only if the stains showed up too much. Madam would get angry if they changed their bedding too often because she said it took a few days for everything to dry, and soiled bedding was better than no bedding at all. She took pride in making sure they all bathed every day, so even if the bedding wasn't clean, at least her girls were. She would then sweep the floor and tidy up the room so that she'd be ready, after her meal and wash, to accept anyone who was escorted to her room. The bed was the main focus of the room, along with a sideboard upon which sat a chipped washbasin filled with fresh water. Mildrea changed this water out daily so she could clean herself between clientele. Some of the other women didn't bother to change or refill theirs and would often get into trouble when one of Madam's spies reported them. There was also a clothing stand made of rough wood to hold her three dresses and a few candles to light her dingy room.

Entering the communal bathing area was the highlight of the day because at least there you could speak to some of the other women and try to forget what you did. Here you could learn which village the women came from and how they got caught up in this lifestyle. Mildrea found it hard to believe that some of them had actually chosen this, and she pitied those who had been born into it and knew of no other way to survive. Still, there were others who had been sent here by their families because they couldn't afford to feed them and thought this would be best. She wondered if their families had ever been to a brothel and seen the things these women had to do. Would they not have tried to come up with another solution?

She thought back to the first day she walked through the castle grounds and saw the women, with their children running and playing, hanging laundry. Such a fool she had been to think these women were leading decent lives. They were just like her, and the children she saw playing were the innocent outcome of what they did for a living. Pity the little girls because they would most likely end up in the same line of work as their mothers. The boys might get away, although she did hear about some young boys and men, in another part of the castle, who did pretty much the same thing as she did because that's what some men and women wanted for their pleasure.

Certain women Mildrea avoided. She remembered how they had treated her with contempt on her first morning of entering the communal bathing room. They were older, used up, and jealous of her youth. One of them had even accused her of thinking she was better than them and threatened her if she were to lose any of her regulars to her. She told Mildrea, "Don't be thinking you're better than me. It wouldn't take much to mess up your pretty little face with a sharp blade."

She stayed out of their way as best as she could and made a point of trying to befriend any new girls who found themselves here, those who seemed shocked, just as she had been, nearly three summers ago. She remembered how it had all seemed like a nightmare and thought that if they found one person who was kind to them, it might make their transition a little bit easier. She would tell them to cooperate because if they fought too much or tried to escape, the beatings were horrible. One woman was barely recognizable after being beaten. Even after the cuts and bruises had healed, her nose was always crooked, and her arm bent out in an awkward way because the break had never been taken care of. The other women were told not to go near her or help her unless they wanted the same thing to happen to them. One day, she was no longer there, and Mildrea believed she had died or possibly even been killed because she was no longer popular with any men.

It hadn't taken her long to realize that as long as you fawned over the man in your room, lying to him and pretending that he was the best man you'd ever been with, he would usually be satisfied. Most of them anyway. There were a few who seemed to find great pleasure in slapping her around a bit. It aroused them. At first, she had been so surprised and frightened that she just cried out and tried to protect herself, but before too long, with one extremely rough client, she decided enough was enough, and after climbing off the bed to get away from him, she ran to her dresser and grabbed her chipped washbasin. Smashing it on the dresser, it broke into several pieces, and she was left with a shard of very sharp porcelain in her hand. He was laughing at her anger and walked towards her, taunting her with words. As he raised his hand to strike her, Mildrea slashed out with the shard and cut him across the cheek. Blood poured from his cheek, and he grabbed his clothes and stormed out of the room, cursing her. Word got around that she was feisty and not to be knocked about. Madam was angry, as she had to refund the man and told Mildrea that she would take it out of her earnings. This made no difference to Mildrea because she barely received any money, nothing regular at least. She had no idea how much was paid for time spent with her, nor did she care.

Although Madam had feigned anger over the money, she said, "I know that not all of my girls enjoy roughhousing as much as others, so if that isn't to your liking, I'll try to steer those men to some of the others who do like it. Besides, I don't want my merchandise damaged. You're one of the prettier ones, and I'd like to keep it that way. I can charge a bit more for you, for a while at least." Then Madam had laughed and walked away down the dark hallway, leaving a trail of her sweet odorous scent behind her.

A few days later, Mildrea walked outside after she'd tidied up, eaten, and bathed, as she still had a little time before her workday would begin. It was a beautiful spring morning with glorious sunshine, blue skies, and a few wispy clouds floating by. She leant upon a wall and closed her eyes, listening to birdsong and imagining what it would be like to fly. For a much too brief moment, she forgot the living hell that was her life. When she opened her eyes, she noticed a man watching her. She was used to being groaked at, yet this was different, this man wasn't looking at her in that way, but in an almost kind way, and he smiled a shy smile and then turned and walked away. A few small items were spilling from his bag, and even a book dropped out. Mildrea hurriedly picked up the book and started to go after him then stopped as she decided he wouldn't want to talk to her. She was just one of the many prostitutes around, so why would he bother speaking to her? She took the book back to her room and got on with her day and night of work.

Over the next few weeks, things slowed down a bit. The king had sent many of his men away from the castle on a scouting expedition to the villages, and they had fewer visitors. This was a much-needed break for the women, and Mildrea spent a lot of time sitting in the sun, reading the book the stranger had dropped. She wished she had been a better pupil when her mother was teaching her to read, but she was able to read most of the words. She finished it and wondered if she would ever see the man again to return his book and thank him for breaking up her tedious, awful existence.

One bright morning, just as she was about to sit in her favorite spot, she spied the kind stranger. She decided to risk it and go talk to him. If any of Madam's spies reported back to her that Mildrea was speaking with someone outside, she would say she was simply enticing him to come and pay her a visit later. Speaking to outsiders was mostly frowned upon, in case it encouraged anyone to leave, but if it might mean money in the coffers, then surely Madam would approve.

"Excuse me, sir, you dropped a book a few weeks ago. I wonder if you might have another to trade for it?"

The man recognized the young lady from a month ago. He had observed her enjoying the sun and thought she was quite lovely, yet when she opened her eyes to look at him, he saw an awful sadness and wondered if she was one of the working women from the brothel. Many times, they had come on to him, saying coarse things he would've been embarrassed to repeat to his wife, yet this woman was different. She looked almost guilty to be making eye contact, and even now when she was speaking to him, there was no flirtatious manner in her speech or the way she had walked toward him. Perhaps he had been mistaken in thinking her a prostitute.

"Oh, I wondered what had happened to that book. You have it, you say?"

Mildrea just looked at him. It had been a long time since she had looked at any man without spite, and here she was having a conversation with someone who seemed decent and not interested in her for her body. "Yes, I have it and I will return it. I just... I just wondered if you might have another one for me. Reading helps break up my day, a bit," she said, as she nodded toward the brothel.

Thomas was struck by the innocence peeking through her rough exterior. She really was just a child, quite a few years younger than his wife Eleanor. "Of course, I can bring you another one. Any particular request?"

At this, Mildrea smiled and bowed her head. "No request, just something to read. I'll bring your book outside for you when next you are here. When will that be?" she asked.

"Oh, I usually come to the castle every two weeks. Will that be all right?"

Mildrea nodded yes and turned to go back to sit down.

Thomas stepped forward and said, "Excuse me, my name is Thomas. May I know your name?"

Ever since the day Creavy had orally raped her, Mildrea hadn't told anyone her name. She looked at this kind stranger and, for the first time since leaving home, she said, "My name is Mildrea, but everyone here calls me Rose. That's the only name I go by now. Mildrea is from another life. I'll see you in a fortnight, and I'll have your book with me." She turned and walked away.

Thomas wanted to follow her but thought better of it. He wondered who she was, what her story was. Perhaps he would find out another time. He returned home to his wife, yet the girl preyed heavily on his mind.

8

After what seemed like weeks, Blythe and Waleda came upon a village, just awakening from its slumber. The people didn't pay much attention to them when they arrived around sunrise one morning. They were living in fear of greeting strangers and weren't interested in knowing anything going on outside of their own village. There had been a time when an outsider was greeted with warmth and curiosity about any news from elsewhere. Since King Traintor's reign, a deadly disease of silence had spread throughout Welexia. Waleda approached a woman emptying a chamber pot beside her house and asked where she might find an herbalist or an apothecary. The woman wouldn't even look at her as she tossed the contents of the pot away and turned quickly to go back indoors, slamming the door behind her.

There was a farmer milking a cow outside of his shed, so she approached him. He said, "We don't want no trouble. You'd best keep walking."

"I don't want any trouble either, but if I don't find an herbalist for my husband, I fear he will die. Please, won't you tell me if someone in this village is a healer?"

The only response she received was the sound of the milk hitting the insides of the bucket as he continued to squeeze the udders, so she persisted, "At least tell me if there is an apothecary where I might obtain some tinctures."

He didn't look at her, but his head nodded toward a structure across the road.

"Thank you," she said as she walked back to Blythe and gently led Kindness and him to where she hoped to find a miracle cure for her husband. She had kept his wounds as clean as possible whilst traveling, but he seemed to have an infection. He burned with fever and had not healed the way she'd hoped. His wounds had scabbed over, but she feared the poison was trapped inside of them, festering away. She punctured one and squeezed out the thick oozing gunk until Blythe cried out and begged her to stop, and then he fell into a fitful sleep. When she saw the wound had swelled up again the next day, she knew it was beyond her skills to cure him.

Tying Kindness up to a post, she walked towards the doorway. The door was ajar, so she peeked inside and saw an older person seated at a work table of sorts. Their hair was long and grey and matted into chunks. There were bits of bark and plant debris tucked into it, almost decoratively so. She wasn't sure if they were male or female, and even after they spoke, she still didn't know.

In a croaky voice, and without looking up from the bird they appeared to be dissecting, they said, "Well, are you going to come in or just spend the day gawking at me?"

Taken aback and a little embarrassed, she replied, "If it pleases you, I would like to come in and seek your assistance." As the person turned their face towards her, she noticed both eyes were milky and clouded over with blindness. She had approached their door very quietly and wondered how they had known she was there.

As if reading her mind, they said, "I smelled you, your horse, and your infected other being when you came into the village. When your smell became stronger, I knew you had arrived at my door."

Deciding to draw upon her inner strength, Waleda stepped over the threshold and said, "Well, if you smelled us and know that my husband has an infection, do you have something that I can use to cure him? I can pay you in household items, as we don't seem to have much need for them anymore, being that we no longer have a house."

They grumbled a bit, got up, and gathered bits of God only knows, including a pestle and mortar, and started grinding something that smelled putrid into a paste.

Feeling in the way and not even sure if whatever they were making had anything to do with her request, Waleda stepped outside to check on Blythe.

His breathing was shallow, and he could barely speak, but he opened his eyes and weakly said, "Waleda, don't you waste anything that we own on trying to fix me up. I've had a long life, a good life with you. I'm only sorry that I am leaving this earth knowing that you will be on your own, without our children, or even a home. I tried to be a good husband to you, and I'm sorry that I failed you. I love you, and when you find Mildrea, tell her I love her also."

"No, no, Blythe, you are not leaving me today. Do you hear me? You will not leave me. We have made it this far, we will keep going together. Please, please, don't go, please, don't go."

A voice croaked behind her, "He's already gone, my dear. That is why I didn't make you anything.

I smelled his death and knew there was nothing I could do for him." Then they placed a gnarly hand upon her arm and said, "Come inside. We will arrange for him to be buried or burned, whichever you prefer. There is nothing more to be done."

Jerking away, she screamed, "You don't understand. He's all I have left in this world."

Waleda had held in her grief for Farnsly because their survival depended on her strength, but now she let the pain and anger out, sobbing uncontrollably, not caring if she awoke everyone in the whole damned village. She wailed from deep within and held on to her dear Blythe's body, fearing that if she let go of him she would fall into a bottomless dark hole of despair.

Eventually she decided burning Blythe's body and scattering his ashes was the best thing to do. She also didn't have the strength to bury him by herself, and as no one in the village seemed inclined to help apart from Healer, it made the most sense. Healer led her to a place where they could burn his body and suggested she gather up some of his ashes to keep upon her person as a talisman for protection. They also said they would like some of them to keep, as the ashes of someone who was loved were very powerful in healing remedies. She agreed to all of this, and after a few days of sitting nearby or returning to add more wood to keep a fire burning underneath him, Blythe's body was burnt to ash and a few bone fragments. She solemnly scooped up some ashes, for Healer and herself, and through her tears felt a contentment that was almost therapeutic.

Healer suggested she stay with them for a while, cleaning, and writing down all of the remedies that were being made up. They explained they wanted a record of everything to pass down to someone who might be willing to learn. "Perhaps that someone is you," they said.

The work was rewarding. It felt good to be settled in a permanent place after being on the run for so long. After her morning chores, she would deliver pouches of herbs and other concoctions to villagers in exchange for food for Healer and herself. The villagers weren't any friendlier, but they accepted she was there to stay, and they liked the personal delivery. It meant they didn't have to go themselves to Healer's ofttimes smelly abode.

Although it was much cleaner than it used to be, there were so many dead creatures and pungent plants that there was a permanent odor in the air. Waleda kept sprigs of lavender and other fragrant plants all around, especially in the corner where her sleeping cot resided. She thought some of the villagers were frightened of her, especially the children. She couldn't really blame them, as she had let her silver hair grow long and taken to tying various items from nature into it as well. Mostly lavender, but if she found a pretty feather, it was added to her mane. This, along with the loosely fitted woolen dresses she wore, the company she kept, the knife attached to her waist, and the songs she sang as she walked through the village and the woods gathering plants and putting them into her assortment of pouches, also tied around her waist, must've made her appear a little touched or crazy.

"Off with the faeries" is what her nan would say when she was a young girl daydreaming. After all that had happened in her life, the faeries seemed like good company.

One summer day, after a full cycle of seasons, one of the king's men rode into the village. He came to Healer's cottage to get something for his son, who had fallen ill with a fever and a rash. He needed some way to heal him. Clearly this man was desperate and was taking a risk because all peasant remedies had been outlawed by King Traintor. Reluctant at first, Healer pleaded ignorance to what was being asked, but after much cajoling and some gold coins being placed on the table, they told Waleda to hand over a pouch from the shelf, and then they gave explicit directions to the man for how to administer it.

"You must use it only as I say, too much and it will kill him. This is a very powerful mixture," said Healer.

The man hurried away. It didn't seem he had listened to either the directions or the warning as he mounted his horse and rode off.

A week later, Healer shook Waleda from a deep sleep. The moon was full, allowing her to see the fear upon their face. She also heard an urgency in their voice that she'd never heard before.

"Wake up, Waleda, you must run into the woods and hide." Then they handed her a bundle of most of their remedies, mixing bowls, and tools. "Hurry, there isn't much time."

"But what about you?" she said.

"I must stay here and try to convince them that there is only me. If they remember you and try to come after you, they will kill you also. I've lived many years, experienced birth, death, drought, happiness, hatred, and even some joy. You still have time to get away. Go... Find your daughter. You may still be able to save her."

"My daughter? What do you know of my daughter?"

"I know she is at the castle, and she needs your help. Now run."

Waleda was running out the back towards the woods as the horses came galloping through the village. They stopped in front of Healer's cottage, and there was much shouting. Hiding from the full moon behind a bush, she watched in horror as soldiers dragged Healer out of the house and began beating them. She recognized the leader as the king's man who had gotten medicine for his son and could hear him shouting that Healer was a devil and their evil potions had killed his son. No one in the village came to help. Healer, who had cured them of so many ailments, saved so many lives, was now alone and helpless.

Waleda wanted to run back and attack all of the king's men but knew that any one of them would knock her down with a sword in one swipe and kill her. There was nothing she could do, so she cowered behind the bush, listening to the sickening sound of someone being beaten to death, waiting for them to leave.

As the sun was rising, Healer finally died and the cruel men left, taking Waleda's horse, Kindness, with them. Gathering up her new bundle, she went to look upon Healer one more time. It didn't feel right leaving them there to become carrion for wild animals, so she dragged the body into the home where they had lived together and been happy. She laid them out on her bed, lit all of the oily rags and torches to be found, and left them to be cremated with their plants and potions. It was midmorning by the time she had finished, and still no one came to see what had happened.

Knowing this village was now her past, she walked through the wet grass into the woods as a nomad on the run yet again. Only this time, she was completely alone. She wondered how Healer had known anything of Mildrea. When she'd first arrived, she told the story of her son being murdered and going on the run with Blythe, but there had been no discussion of her family since then. Her hope was that Mildrea was working in the castle kitchens, living a decent life. Now, based on the second sight of Healer, she feared her daughter needed her and decided to go to the castle and find her.

9

Mildrea had asked Thomas for something to write with, a piece of charcoal or a sharpened stick and some ink. She wanted to write a letter to her parents and brother and asked him if he would be so kind as to deliver it. She could write it on a piece of cloth, but she had nothing to write with. Madam made sure the women had very few personal items. Her village was a bit further from the castle than his, but Thomas said he could make an extra trip and try to sell some of his goods there, so he would gladly deliver her letter.

When he arrived at the village, he noticed how still and quiet it was. It looked abandoned. It was certainly run down. Then he noticed a few women and children near some of the houses. Slowly making his way towards them, he asked if they'd like to buy any of his goods. They said they had no money but when the men returned from the fields later, they might be interested in some of his tools.

"Thank you, I'll do that. Would you point me to where Blythe and Waleda live, please?"

One of the women said, "You'd best not be askin' about them. You can wait for the menfolk if you like, but no more questions."

He walked over to a tree to sit in the shade and eat. Eleanor had packed him some fruit, nuts, fresh barley bread, and a lump of cheese for his meal. He waited, hoping the men would be more talkative.

When the men returned, the women pointed to him, and a few of them came over to inspect what he was peddling. Thomas could see these were dirt-poor farmers by their ragged clothes and shoes, and he knew they didn't have money enough between them to buy anything. Being no fool, he also knew they might try to rob him. He'd encountered this before, much more often since King Traintor was in power, so he always kept his large knife strapped to his waist and his tools tied to his cart for an easy getaway.

He began gathering everything up and told them he had other villages to get to, places where people would buy and not just look. Then he said he'd be back tomorrow with more variety for them to choose from as he climbed onto his cart and took the horse's reins in his hands. The men grumbled a bit but didn't seem to have energy for a tussle. On top of this, they were overworked and malnourished. Thomas, tall and fit, could easily take any of them down.

"Before I leave, might you be able to tell me where Blythe and Waleda live?"

Like scattering insects, they quickly scurried away. No one said anything, they just disappeared into their homes. He noticed one man hanging back, underneath the overhang of an outbuilding. This man seemed healthier than the rest, and Thomas thought he might have some trouble fighting him off easily.

Making sure to look him directly in the eye as he passed, he nodded to the man, to let him know he'd seen him, and as he rode by, the stranger said, "Meet me at the edge of the village, and I'll have some answers for you."

It could be a trap, but Thomas decided to take a chance. He'd come this far, and he was curious as to why no one would talk to him. The way Mildrea had described her village, it sounded like a very nice community. She had also spoken of many friends. Besides, he would like to deliver her letter and bring back news of her family. Once at the village edge, Thomas climbed down from his cart and waited for the stranger to arrive. He noticed several burial mounds, more than there should be for a small village like this. The stranger approached and looked around nervously as he walked over to one of the mounds and gestured for Thomas to join him. Seeing no others around, Thomas walked cautiously and slowly forward.

"I hear you're asking about some people. This is where young Farnsly is buried. I buried him myself," the stranger said.

Taken aback, Thomas asked, "And his parents?"

"They disappeared."

"What do you mean they disappeared?"

The man nervously looked around again before saying, "Rumor has it they ran off in the middle of the night, after their son had a terrible accident."

He watched Thomas's face closely to see if there might be any recognition of the kind of accident that had befallen young Farnsly. When Thomas looked puzzled, Gyles said, "He was murdered, same as most of the people buried here, by the king's men. That's why no one here will talk to you. They think you might be a spy, working for the king."

"I'm no spy, just a friend of Mildrea, and she asked me to deliver a note to her parents. That's the only reason I'm here," Thomas said, as he produced a rolled up bit of cloth from his pouch.

Gyles sensed he was sincere and introduced himself and asked about Mildrea. He wanted to know if she was working in the kitchens at the castle and if she was faring well. Thomas felt no need to lie to this man who had been truthful with him, so he shook his head and said that, although the letter he was carrying described an idyllic life, she was not doing well. She had been trapped into working for someone inside the castle, and she had no way of getting away, as she had no money and, just like the king's spies who came to this village, there were many of them keeping a close watch upon her. He said the only reason he was able to speak to her was because he could come and go from within the castle walls carrying the goods he sold. And since he and Mildrea always spoke out in the open, they managed to develop a friendship, and no one suspected anything else.

Gyles shook his head and said he was sorry to hear this. He had been friends with the family. He didn't know where Waleda and Blythe had gotten to, but he knew Blythe had terrible injuries when they left. And since they left with only one horse and whatever they could carry on the night their son had died, he wasn't even sure they were still alive. He then described to Thomas that sad day and explained how he promised them he would bury Farnsly and had done so. Thomas asked him if there was any message he wanted delivered to Mildrea.

Gyles replied, "Just tell her hello from me, and tell her that if she does ever manage to make it back home, I'll be here and gladly take her in, as a daughter, until her parents return. If they ever do."

Thomas thanked him and told Gyles his name. He also said he might return another day if he heard anything else about Blythe, Waleda, or Mildrea. He rode off before darkness overtook them completely, as he wanted to get home safely to Eleanor. Since she knew nothing of his friendship with Mildrea, he had only told her he was heading out to some other villages to sell tools and that he may return a day later than when he went only to the castle. Although he told her not to worry, he knew she would. She always did. It was just her way.

As he rode home, he wondered how he would tell Mildrea what he had learned about her family. She deserved the truth, but he knew how heartbroken she would be. Whenever she spoke of home, it was with a fondness, a fondness she hadn't appreciated when she lived there. Now she wished, more than ever, to be home with her family. She didn't think they'd want her back if they knew of her situation, but Thomas could tell her that Gyles had offered to care for her if she came home. He hoped this would give her the encouragement she needed to escape. And he knew deep down that, although he would be risking his life, he would even assist her in doing so, if that was what she wanted to do.

10

One morning in the bath house, Mildrea realized, at twenty summers old, she was now considered one of the older working women in the brothel. There were some men who favored women with experience if they still looked pretty good and had no children, but this life certainly took its toll on their looks, and it was rare to not have given birth after a few years.

This was something Mildrea had been determined never to do, and she had most likely permanently damaged herself the two times she had chosen to terminate a pregnancy. The first time, she ate a pungent root given to her by another working woman, which caused extreme cramping and vomiting, but it had worked. Having no root available the second time she knew she was with child, she inserted a very sharp thin metal rod inside her and poked around through her tears and anger at what she was doing. Both were immensely painful experiences, physically and emotionally, and as she bled out, she was certain she would die. She had to lie to Madam and tell her she was having a heavy flow during her moon cycle and needed a few days in bed. Two days were all Madam ever allowed anyone to be out of commission, so even in excruciating pain, and whilst still eliminating her fetus, she had returned to receiving customers. She had no choice.

If she was sterile, it didn't matter to her. She was resigned to a miserable life, never to find love with anyone. She hated most of the men, and who would want her after her years working in the brothel? Some of the other women talked about how they were going to be taken away by their special clients who promised marriage, but Mildrea had yet to see this become a reality for any of them. More often than not, they would take their own lives instead of bearing the humility any longer. It had crossed her mind a few times, especially after Thomas reported back to her that no one knew where her parents were and that her brother had been murdered. Still, Gyles had made his kind offer, and she was hopeful that perhaps she would one day be freed from her life of hell. Maybe King Traintor would be ousted and she might escape then. Either that or the men would want her less and less, and Madam would find a way to make her disappear as she had done with so many others.

Over the years, Mildrea figured out that Madam paid Creavy for bringing her fresh young girls and continued to get a percentage of their earnings. The busier those girls were, the more money he got, which is why he wanted Mildrea to always be working. His visits with her were gratis, of course, and he took complete advantage of that, spending longer with her than any of her other clients dared.

Madam would, quite literally, come barging into the room and drag a man from on top of a woman if he was taking too long or had fallen asleep. And although she never did this with Creavy, one day she hadn't realized he was in the room with Mildrea when she came bursting through the door. He paused, smiled at her, and invited her to join them. She laughed and said she wasn't interested in that but agreed to stay and watch the fun. She sat in the corner moaning, whilst Mildrea turned away and stared at the wall, even more ashamed than usual. As Creavy heaved away, she turned her head and looked in Madam's direction to find that Madam wasn't watching Creavy, she was watching Mildrea. Madam licked her lips and parted her mouth a little as she panted and stared at her until Creavy finally reached his climax. Then she rose and walked out, telling Creavy not to take too much longer. There were others waiting for their special girl.

A few days later, there was a knock on her door. It was one of Madam's servants, saying Madam wished to see Mildrea in her private chamber. They added that Madam wished Mildrea to wear her hair up on her head and to put on the dress the servant was now handing her. It was a flattering style but made of cheap fabric, and it reeked of Madam's sickly sweet smell.

When Mildrea hesitated, the servant shook their head and said, "It's best to do as she says, Rose. Her temper is unforgiving." Then they brushed their hand upon the huge scar that ran from their eyebrow down to the corner of their mouth. "I'll be back to collect you soon." With that, they turned and left.

Puzzle pieces fell into place. Madam had several young women servants, all with scarred faces. Mildrea often wondered where they'd all come from. Now she knew. She began to dress herself and pile her hair on top of her head.

She was pacing back and forth in her room when the servant returned, saying she looked beautiful. Mildrea allowed herself a small smile and thanked them. Then she reached out and touched their forearm, asking what was going to happen. Looking down and shaking their head, the servant simply turned, indicating she should follow.

Walking down the dimly lit corridor had never felt right to Mildrea. Even after four miserable winters in this place, it made her feel queasy whenever she neared Madam's room. She always smelled Madam before she saw her, and now, even the dress she was wearing held the repulsive scent of this monstrous little woman. This time, they walked straight past the office and into another room with much more light. Mildrea had never seen so many candles in one room before. The servant bowed and then scurried away.

Madam was seated on a settee, sipping a dark liquid from a beautiful glass, like those Mildrea had seen outside the castle when she first arrived. She motioned for Mildrea to sit in a chair opposite her, then she stood and poured another drink and handed it to her. She smiled, showing the few teeth left amongst the rotten ones hanging on for dear life inside her mouth.

Mildrea, out of fear from what the servant said, shyly smiled back, took the drink, and bowed her head.

Madam reached out and grasped her chin, pulling her head up and looking her straight in the eye. "You will do exactly as I say. You will not tell anyone what happens in this room, especially Creavy. And should I be pleased, you will return whenever I say so. If you fail me in any way, you will disappear. Do I make myself clear?"

"Yes," Mildrea uttered, barely audible.

"You are one of my more intelligent girls, so do not try to trick me in any way. Just do as I say, and you will be fine." Madam then released Mildrea's face and told her to drink the liquid.

It took everything not to cry, but she didn't want this vile woman to know just how frightened and sickened she felt in her presence so she drank. And waited...

After another glass each, Madam got out a pipe and began smoking something. This was the pungent sweet smell that Mildrea always smelled. She felt lightheaded and odd as the room became smokier. Madam then patted the seat beside her, and Mildrea slowly rose and crossed the room to sit down next to this woman who held her life in her hands. She shouldn't have been shocked but still gasped out loud when Madam slowly slid her hand underneath her dress and began touching her inner petals and encircling her clitoris with her gnarly fingers.

"See how nice this feels. I bet none of the men who come to you make you feel this nice. Only I can do it. Pay careful attention to what I'm doing." Then she put her fingers directly on top of the throbbing area and applied some pressure.

Midrea was disgusted that this woman was touching her. Perhaps it was the alcohol and the smoke in the room, but she found herself feeling slightly aroused, and she hated herself for it.

Then, just as suddenly as it had begun, Madam stopped what she was doing. "Now, do it to me, just the way I showed you. Do it. Now!" Madam barked as she raised her skirt up to her waist, exposing herself.

Feeling no longer aroused and now only sickened, Mildrea got onto the floor and began touching Madam just how she had been touched, as best she could. Madam reached down and took her hand and began guiding it. Then she took a large smooth wooden object that looked like a penis from the side table and told Mildrea to suck on it and get it nice and wet. Once done, she took it from her and, closing her eyes, inserted it into herself.

Now opening her eyes, she said, "Move it in and out of me. Fuck me with it, but don't stop what you're doing with your other hand." Then she placed both of her hands on Mildrea's head and began undoing her hair, spilling it upon her shoulders. Madam was moaning and writhing around, making it difficult for Mildrea to keep up her tasks. Mildrea was removing herself from her body, just as she did whenever men were sent to her room.

She always felt filthy sick with herself whenever she had to be with any of these men, and now was no different. She knew some of the other women had found loving relationships with each other, comforting and pleasuring one another, and she understood that. This was nothing like that. This was just like any other of the forced sexual encounters she had been doing for the last four years of her life, but Madam had threatened to make her disappear if she didn't please her, so this time, she was doing it to live.

Mildrea was relieved when Madam finally spasmed and released her head. Wiping her hands upon the cheap fabric dress she was wearing, she hoped she would be allowed to return to her own room soon.

"Oh yes, yes, yes, yes, yes, that was even better than I thought, my dear. I wasn't sure you had it in you, Rose. Oh, Creavy always says you are special. This time, I agree with him. You've done well. I will keep you on, but only as long as you please me. I've many other things to teach you about pleasuring a woman. We've only just begun. I can hardly wait. It makes me moist just thinking about it. You'll be eating out of my palms when I'm finished with you, begging me for more. You may find that hard to believe, but it has happened before. You shall see."

Mildrea drank the drink offered and sat back down in her chair, feeling nauseous.

"How do you think I came to be at the head of this business? I started out where you were. I was forced to sleep with those despicable men every day. I hated them. My madam brought me here and taught me ways to please her. I pleased her so much, so very much, just like you will continue to please me. Then, one day, I pleased her beyond her wildest dreams and took over the business."

Mildrea choked on her wine and nearly spat it out when hearing this. Madam tilted her head back and laughed.

Sleep did not come that night, as the time was taken up trying to figure out just how she could get away from this place. She thought her life had been miserable before, but now it was worse than she ever imagined it could be. Over the next few months, Madam held true to her word, sending for Mildrea and teaching her more ways to pleasure her. Always the same, always by demonstrating first. As much as she hated touching Madam, she hated even more being touched by her. When Creavy had first sample-tasted her, assaulting her, she was mortified and shocked, and now Madam was doing the same thing. She was doing things to Mildrea that she knew nothing about, things the men had never done to her. Madam was quite fond of having things inserted into her anus, so this meant Mildrea must first learn how it felt and how best to do it.

Just as with the men, she began pretending she enjoyed all that was happening. This seemed to please Madam, and Mildrea found that if she was pleased, she let Mildrea leave sooner. Instead of staying on and talking about how wonderful everything had felt, she said she was tired and wanted to go to sleep. Mildrea also used her visits to the inner chamber to look around. She began paying attention to where things were kept, all of the sex toys, the alcohol, the drugs, and she even saw some money. Not a lot of money, but enough to get away from the castle. She knew she must bide her time though and carefully plan her escape because she would only get one chance. If she failed, she would be killed. Of this, she had no doubt.

Creavy was still a regular, and as long as he desired her, she was most likely to remain amongst Madam's stable. At least that's what he believed. He had no idea that her pleasing Madam was why she was kept around. Creavy was truly disgusting. He rarely bathed, he never rinsed out his mouth, and his breath smelled like rotten cabbage. Mildrea had done everything she could to convince him that he would find more pleasure with someone else. She never smiled, never laughed at his jokes, never pretended to be enjoying herself like she did with others. She simply laid there and let him find his own pleasure. Nothing worked. It actually seemed to excite him and make him want her more.

One day, he told her to urinate on him whilst he pounded away at her. She tried for ages to make herself do so, but it just wasn't happening. He laughed and said he could bang into her all day if need be, but he wasn't going away until she had done it. Between his erections, when he would pull out of her, he insisted she masturbate or suck his cock. Just before he came, he would begin fucking her again, pulling her hair and telling her to piss on him. She was on top and bearing down so hard, trying to force herself to pee, that instead she shat all over him.

Bracing herself to be smacked across the face, she was shocked when Creavy, instead of being disgusted, thought this was a wonderful sensation and told her he may have just found a new favorite way to get off with her. Mildrea was strong and hadn't cried in front of Creavy except for on her first day, but being humiliated by both him and Madam was too much, and she broke down.

He loved it and talked sweetly to her saying, "There, there, don't you cry. Creavy will always be 'ere for you. You and I 'ave a special bond. Madam knows that. That's why she's promised to keep you around just as long as I like. Fortunately for you, I think you've a few good years left in you yet, and I aim to be your special date as often as I'm around."

Hearing these words, something snapped in Mildrea. She stopped crying and began cleaning herself up, almost trance like. Creavy, of course, thought his words had comforted her and kissed her on the neck.

Fully composed and lying she said, "Please take me to see Madam. I want to tell her that you should always be given preference over my other clients, as I now know you're my favorite."

"Oh darlin', you know I will, but later today. First, clean up your shit-soaked bed and ready yourself for the next paying customer. Creavy 'as bills to pay." Then he kissed her roughly and left.

II

Thomas was wondering how much longer he would visit the castle. People weren't buying things the way they used to. They were so angry with each other. He often saw fighting, even amongst those he'd thought were friends before. Taking a break to eat his lunch, he began wondering where Mildrea was. He hadn't noticed her around the last two times he'd been there and was worried about her. He must be careful asking after her though, as he didn't want to get her into trouble. He saw a man enter the castle through the side door Mildrea used, telling his friend to wait for him. Thomas decided to take a chance and walked over to the friend.

Tossing him an apple, he said, "Hello friend, the wife packed me two of these today."

"Cheers."

"I'm Thomas, pleasure to meet you."

Eyeing him suspiciously, he replied, "Jonesy."

"Jonesy, I notice you're friends with the tall chap. The one who just entered the castle. He looks familiar to me. Mind telling me his name?"

"'is name's Creavy, but 'e'll be none too pleased when I tell 'im you is asking after 'im."

"I mean no harm, friend, just thought he looked familiar. Obviously, I was mistaken. Well, best be on my way."

Not wanting to stick around until Creavy returned, knowing Jonesy would point him out, Thomas gathered up his wares onto his cart. He tried to make it look leisurely, so as not to arouse any more suspicion in his new acquaintance and nodded his head as he departed. Once he'd gone about half a furlong from the castle walls, he rented some space in a nearby barn for his cart and paid the landowner to keep his wares safe, promising him he could choose an item for himself and his wife upon his return if nothing had gone missing. He then rode his horse back towards the castle, finding a spot amongst the trees to wait. He wanted to find out what Creavy and Jonesy were all about and what they may know about Mildrea. He hoped Eleanor wouldn't worry too much if he was away from home for a few nights. It happened every so often when he was working.

As night fell, he saw the two men leaving the castle. They had a few words, and then Jonesy headed in one direction and Creavy another. Better to approach Creavy when he was alone. He was tall and wiry, but Thomas still had about four stone in weight over him and thought he'd come out on top in a scrap. He was hoping that wouldn't occur but made sure his knife would easily come out of its strap, should the need arise.

After a time, while Thomas was following at a safe distance behind Creavy, the sun set. It grew dark quickly, and he chided himself for not finding a safe spot off the road for the night earlier. He had just dismounted his horse and headed into the trees when he heard another animal snort behind him. Turning around, he saw Creavy sitting atop his horse just before he felt a thud on the side of his head, knocking him to the ground. Momentarily confused, he fumbled around for his knife that had flown off into the grass. Creavy jumped off his horse and lunged on top of him. Thomas used his larger size to flip Creavy onto his back for the advantage. He also saw the moonlight flash upon his knife blade on a mound of earth nearby but knew reaching for it might allow Creavy a chance to wriggle out from underneath him. He decided to do it anyway, and when he grabbed for the knife, Creavy slithered off in the opposite direction. They each faced off to one another with about two meters between them.

"Why is you followin' me?"

"I just want to ask you some questions, about Mil... about Rose?"

"What da fuck do you know about Rose?"

"I just want to know if she's alright. I haven't seen her around for a while. She and I are friends. Well, not really friends. I bring her books to read in her... in her... free time."

Something about this struck Creavy as hilarious, and he began to laugh. "Yeah, well, she ain't got a lot of free time. Except when she's underneaf me. She's always free for me."

Thomas's rage took over, and he threw all of himself at this scrawny, slimy man, at once overpowering him and getting him on the ground, with his knife blade at his throat. "Now, tell me what's happened to Rose or my knife might just slip, just a little bit, you piece of shite."

Creavy was a survivor and knew when he'd been beaten. "Alright, alright, no need to get so angry. I will tell you whatever you want to know. Just ease up a bit, yeah?"

"Not likely. Talk first." Thomas hadn't realized how tense he had become worrying about Mildrea until this moment. It wasn't at all like him to pull a knife on someone. He kept it around for protection, but he knew, at this very moment, that he could kill this man. That frightened him a little.

"She's alright. She's just taken to staying inside more often. She ain't as talkative as she used to be. I don't know what's goin' on wif 'er. Madam says not to worry. I ain't worried. I still fuck 'er whenever I want to, and she still makes me plenty of money wif the other punters. She's just a bit moody is all."

Everything went black for Creavy as Thomas struck him hard across the temple.

Snapping back into reality, Thomas quickly focused on what to do next. He could leave Creavy here, amongst the trees, to slowly regain consciousness, but then he would talk and easily be able to point him out when they were both next inside the castle grounds. Not a good idea. Thomas decided it would be best to use an unconscious Creavy to his advantage and hoisted him up onto his horse. He tied him on so he wouldn't fall off and headed back towards the castle. He wasn't quite sure what he was going to say but knew he'd figure it out before he got there.

As they approached the castle gate, the night watchman hollered out, "Who goes there?"

Thomas pulled his hood over his face, just a little, and said, "I found this man, Creavy, in the woods. He's been attacked. I need to get him inside and get him some medical attention. I know someone will care for him inside the lower castle corridor." Surprisingly, the castle doors creaked open, and Thomas found himself entering and heading straight for Rose's door. Once there, he lifted Creavy off the horse. Creavy moaned, so Thomas struck him again. Keeping him unconscious was the only way he'd not tell the truth about what had happened. He took another chance and rapped upon the door. His adrenalin was soaring when, slowly the door opened to reveal a slight young woman who looked at him blankly for a moment. Then recognizing Creavy, she opened the door completely so Thomas could carry him inside. She indicated Thomas should follow her, and off they went down a dark, dingy corridor.

He had only imagined what the interior of this place looked like and now felt queasy as he knew this was Mildrea's existence. He was led into a room filled with many candles and laid Creavy down on a settee. This was a fancy room, completely the opposite of the hallway they'd just come down. Since the servant had disappeared, he quickly peered out into the hallway and set off himself, going deeper into the labyrinth. He really didn't have a plan, other than he hoped to find Mildrea and help her escape. He had no idea how they'd do this but knew that, since he'd come this far, he must at least try. Before he'd gone two rods, voices started shouting, so he hid in a darkened alcove.

Alerted by her servant, Madam entered her private chambers and saw Creavy collapsed upon her settee. Madam always kept a bucket of water nearby to freshen herself up with. She picked it up and threw the frigid water onto his face. He sputtered and choked from the shock as he sat up. "Whatever has happened that you should be within my inner sanctum?"

Wiping his eyes and shaking the water from his face, Creavy noted she was fuming. He sat up, trying to explain that he had no idea how he'd gotten here. His head throbbed, and his vision was fuzzy. Realization dawned upon him and he said, "There's an intruder inside. We must find 'im. 'e's come for Rose."

12

After seven days, Waleda knew she must be approaching the castle because the roads were filled with many more people. Some as ragged as her, others dressed like lords and ladies. There was only one road in and out of the castle, and both paupers and royalty had to share it. Of course, if a fancy carriage came by or horses and riders carrying flags, the peasants crawled off the road into the ditch until they passed by. A deaf and blind man hadn't done so, simply because he hadn't heard or seen what was happening, and a horseman who belonged to one of the moneyed families cracked him on the skull with a sword and kicked him into the ditch as he passed by. Waleda stood there watching him bleed out and die as everyone else just walked right past. People were somehow numb to this sort of treatment, but it still shocked her and caused much inner pain, knowing they had a king who not only allowed such things to go on but advocated to his followers that it was acceptable. He encouraged such behavior, which sickened her.

She was living off grasses growing on the side of the road and some dried fruit within her bundle. Since she had always slept in her clothes whilst being on the run with Blythe and living with Healer, many pouches were already attached to her waist on the night she was awakened. Within them were some nuts and berries she had gathered on her foraging expeditions. She was grateful she had them. She also knew which dried herbs, from the bundle Healer had given to her, would keep her from feeling hungry and settle her stomach if she ate something that was off, so she was doing relatively well.

One night, she settled under a tree with a family nearby. She always felt safer with families and often sought out groups of people, especially if they had women and children in their party. On this night, one of the women went into labor, and her husband tried to help her, but her cries persisted and she kept screaming that something was wrong with the baby. They weren't far from the castle walls, and Waleda feared someone might come out and silence them all permanently, so she approached and asked if she could help them.

The young man was terrified, as was his even younger wife, so she set him a task of finding something clean within their items to wrap the emerging baby in. She tore up some of the woman's undergarments and told him to go and wash the rags she had made. Then she knelt next to the woman and gave her some bark to chew on. At first, the woman refused. She was verging on delirium, but Waleda spoke softly to her and said it would calm her and her new baby, which would help with the delivery, so she began chewing on it.

Feeling all around her swollen stomach, it was clear to Waleda the baby hadn't turned, and yet the stars, planets, and goddesses had determined it was time for this new life to enter the world. When the husband returned with the washed rags, Waleda explained to him they must get her feet up above her heart to keep the baby within her for just a bit longer. He started piling up everything they had so they could elevate her lower body. Waleda massaged the woman's stomach, trying to get the baby to turn around within her. She knew if it came out either feet first or arse first, there was a very good risk the cord would be caught around the neck, and it might even tear the mother apart. Neither scenario had a good outcome, so she held onto her pouch of Blythe's ashes and said a silent prayer, then she massaged and sang and kept both mother and father calm.

The expectant mother was exhausted, so she was given more dried plants to chew on. What she was given now would also have a numbing effect and take away much of her pain. The baby rested for a while, and Waleda asked if she could reach up inside to find out what the little rascal was up to. Mama nodded, and she proceeded to feel for the baby's head. It was a very dark night, which was a blessing because although Waleda had done this with a cow, she had only ever assisted the midwives in her village when it was time for a human birth. They always handled that, and she simply supported them, doing whatever they asked. Fortunately, the baby was now turning, and Waleda and the father turned the mother around slowly and got her onto all fours, kneeling level upon the ground. She continued to massage her back and gave her another herb to now speed up the labor and delivery.

They hadn't realized people had gathered around them, and as the sun rose, the sounds of a new life entering the world with a piercing scream that pulled the sun up from its slumber caused the crowd to erupt in cheers and laughter. Both the mother and father wept tears of joy. Waleda also cried, grateful and astonished that even in this world so filled with hatred, a new, innocent life could bring so much hope and happiness. On this morning, it felt good to be alive. People shared their food, so everyone ate, and for a while, they were celebrating and being kind to one another. They weren't thinking of yesterday or tomorrow, or survival. They were simply being humans, in the best way possible. After a few hours, and some napping, they all went their separate ways again, putting on their masks of protection. Waleda noted that people had smiled at her for the first time in years, and she was hopeful that they could, just possibly, survive this raving king and the cruel things he said and did.

13

The level of noise and commotion told Thomas his presence was now known, and if he truly wanted to help Mildrea, he must escape and come back another day. He hated leaving her and only wished she knew that he had at least gotten this far.

He pulled his hood up, crouched his body down to appear shorter than he was, waved at someone who came running towards him, and shouted, "He's gone that way!" before heading off in the opposite direction for the door. Once outside, he took his horse into the shadows and hid until things settled down.

He meandered over to the gate and, doing his best to portray an inebriated fellow, begged the night watchman to please let him out or his wife would surely tar and feather him if he didn't get home. The night watchman found him amusing and opened the gate for him to exit. Thomas immediately mounted his horse and rode off into the night as if the hounds of hell were nipping at his heels.

After a restless night sleeping on his cart, he rose the next morning and sorted out payment of goods with the chap who'd kept his word and watched over them. Not quite sure how he could return to the interior castle grounds, he thought he'd best set up shop in the outside market until things calmed down a bit. This way, he could watch out for Creavy and Jonesy and find a way in once they'd left.

As he was watching all who entered and left the castle, he noticed a disheveled, silver-haired woman walking on the road. She was behaving much like him, taking in her surroundings and studying everyone around her. She settled down under a shady tree and began eating something from one of her many bundles. To most observers, she appeared to be napping, but Thomas could tell she was only pretending, as she paid close attention to the castle gates. At one point, she wandered by a cart spilling over with fruit and, with what seemed like a sleight of hand, scooped up a few apples and turnips, which she slipped into one of her pouches before sauntering away. The cart's owner didn't even notice. There was something about this woman that Thomas couldn't quite figure out, but he knew he'd be keeping an eye on her as he waited for Creavy and Jonesy.

A day went by with no sign of either of the men, so Thomas decided to stick around. He was selling quite a few of his items, although at a much reduced rate, and no one seemed to be suspicious of him. Late in the afternoon of the second day, he saw Creavy riding out of the castle gate. He had three other men with him, and they headed off at quite a clip, as if on an important mission. Thomas knew this may be his only chance, and he went down low behind his cart to tinker with something until they'd passed by.

He noticed the silver-haired woman was openly standing in the road staring at Creavy as he rode by as if she too recognized him. Creavy didn't pay any attention to her though. When they'd gone far enough away, Thomas got up and led his horse and cart straight through the gate, the silver-haired woman following him from a safe distance. The woman was swallowed into the crowd of the market.

He looked around for Mildrea but didn't see her anywhere. After a few hours past the time when Mildrea used to come outside, Thomas decided to try and find this other intriguing woman. He didn't know why he wanted to, but something in his gut told him he should, so he set off going from stall to stall, feigning perusal of the merchandise. He knew a few of the stall holders and asked them if they'd seen a funny old silver-haired woman.

"Did I see her?" replied one produce vendor. "Yeah, I saw her. I grabbed her arm when she tried to steal some of me goods. She may look old and haggard, but she's a tough one, she is. She pulled a knife on me, stuck it in me crotch, and threatened to cut me balls off if I shouted and didn't let go of her. As I'm rather attached to me balls, or them to me actually, I told her to go. She went around that corner. I don't expect she'll come near me stall anymore. I shouted after her, saying I'd tell the sheriff if I ever seen her again."

Thomas was surprised and also a little impressed with the spunk of this feisty woman. He knew when someone was simply trying to survive, and he'd seen her steal food before. She was hungry but not quite desperate. She was here for a reason, and he wanted to know what it was. He set off in the direction she'd last been seen, thanking the merchant for the information. "I'd best keep my wits about me if I see her then. Thanks for the warning."

As the afternoon arrived, the interior market became dark with the shadows of the castle walls.

Many vendors started packing up for the day, others only for an afternoon nap and a meal, as they'd be reopening for the evening crowd. This was a different crowd altogether, and Thomas had always gotten away before they came out. They were often drunk and unruly, and only the most experienced market sellers dared to sell to them. He knew he needed to get back to his cart or he'd have nothing left.

As pure darkness enveloped the grounds, torchlight from lanterns and oil-soaked rags began to sparkle intermittently. Some areas would remain in complete darkness until morning, and Thomas thought that was where he should take his cart to rest. He also thought the silver-haired woman was most likely to be in the darkness as well. She didn't want to risk being seen by the man she'd stolen from. Silver hair or not, she was a woman, and women were not safe once the soldiers started drinking. They would rape just about anyone they thought might be vulnerable.

Once he'd found a suitable dark spot, he covered everything up and said a prayer for protection. He allowed his eyes to adjust to the darkness and set about to look for her. There really was something pulling him to her, and he couldn't understand what it was, but he'd always trusted his gut and didn't plan on ignoring it now. Just when he thought his eyes had adjusted pretty well, he tripped over a human bundle who was trying to sleep.

"Oi! That's me leg, you twat! Fuck off!" the disgruntled form cried out.

Quickly stepping back he said, "I'm so sorry, mate. Didn't see you there. I'll be off. Sorry again."

What an awful existence, to be lying in the middle of the dirt, getting trod upon by life, quite literally. This made him think of Eleanor. Right now he wished he was home with her, snuggled up cozily in their warm clean bed. He could almost smell her lavender hair.

Thomas awoke, startled by a goat nibbling on his ear. That's when he saw he'd fallen asleep in an animal pen. He remembered climbing over a low fence in the dark but hadn't realized he had been sleeping with the sheep and goats. Aw well, better than some of the broken humans he had encountered as he searched for a place to rest for the night.

He was just climbing out of the pen when he saw the silver-haired woman coming around the corner. Her shawl was pulled up around her head, but some of her hair had slipped out. He could tell it was her from the many pouches tied around her waist and the way she stuck close to any stalls or buildings as if she didn't want to be seen. He decided to follow her and see where she was going, being careful to watch out for a returning Creavy or Jonesy and getting recognized.

She seemed to sense him and turned to face him unafraid. As the sun rose completely, he saw her face in full sunlight, and it struck him. She actually looked like Mildrea. Her height and body shape were the same, and they even walked similarly. He wondered if this was the mother Mildrea so desperately longed to see. He had no time to ask her, as she turned and darted away, disappearing into a throng of vendors setting up for the day. Not wanting to cause a commotion or attention to himself, he decided to stick to the shadows a while longer until he could make his way over to Mildrea's doorway. He prayed he would see her sunning herself outside so he could speak to her and be sure she was alright. After he had gotten into the castle, he feared for her safety. If they thought she had anything to do with his botched plan, they just might take it out on her.

14

Bracknor had been holed up for four winters. He'd changed his name to Whistler and kept a low profile, creating a past as a farmer from one of the villages that had died out after King Traintor took over the palace. He knew if Newark ever found out he was alive, he'd send his men to kill him. They'd also kill anyone else in the village they thought might be associated with him. For this reason, he was living like a farmer, working the land, blending in, getting to know his neighbors in a village called Vintnos.

He'd even met a woman, a widow named Dandy, and they had become very close. One day, they decided to marry, and an elder of the village obliged them with a handfasting ceremony. This was something Bracknor never thought would happen to him, as his obligations were always to take care of his king.

He settled into the day-to-day living, which wasn't easy. There was rarely enough food to go around the village, but the people of Vintnos cared for each other and wanted to help out their fellow man. He supposed its distance from the castle was the reason they were kinder. They weren't near, so they didn't realize quite how murky things were. Folks around these parts just got on with it. Every so often a group of Newark's men would pass through, roughhousing anyone who didn't acquiesce to them and spewing the king's mandate of hatred, yet the villagers seemed to handle it in their stride. Once they'd gone, things returned to normal. It was almost a game to them.

They felt far enough removed that what happened at the castle didn't really matter to them, until one day when the king's soldiers came through, demanding an increased payment of one quarter of their food stock. Like the other villages, they'd already handed over one sixth of everything they grew and harvested. But payment of this much would mean starvation for many, so their first reaction was to stand up to the men. Once a few of the strongest villagers had been savagely murdered before their eyes, they became silent and let the grains go freely.

Later that night, after King Traintor's men were long gone, a meeting was called in the village hall.

Bracknor, known to everyone in Vintnos as Whistler, seized this opportunity to tell what he knew about King Oshinor, the castle, and the reality of their kingdom. He also revealed that he had, in fact, been the king's right-hand man, a noble, and had been biding his time until he could form an uprising. Once he had spoken, a silence fell about, but then, after some hushed conversations, the villagers said they needed to think about all that had been done to them, and all that Bracknor had said. He could tell some of them were skeptical and doubted what he'd told them about the abduction of King Oshinor. It was easier to believe things weren't as bad as they actually were.

An elder of the village, Manteith, spoke up and said, "We'll deliberate over all that we've heard tonight and meet up tomorrow evening at sunset."

As they dispersed, some men patted Bracknor on the back and gave him knowing nods and words of encouragement. Others wouldn't even make eye contact and steered clear of him. This confirmed his suspicion that he needed to keep watch, lest anyone try to escape and alert King Traintor of his plan during the night.

Once he'd gotten home that evening, his wife greeted him with a very cold shoulder. The women had all been in the village hall and heard everything the men heard.

Some of the women muttered unkind things under their breath. Things like, "Whore, taking in a stranger. I knew he was trouble when he came to our village." Others turned to look at Dandy, to see if she had been in on this the whole time. She stared straight ahead, composed so as not to scream out in shock at the words she was hearing her husband say.

Now that he was home, she daren't say anything, lest she scream and beat him upon the chest. Instead, she slopped some stew into a bowl and then went to the fire to do some mending. The tension in the room was as thick as early morning fog over a pond in winter.

When he could stand the silence no longer, steadying his spoon of stew midway to his mouth, he said, "I couldn't tell you. It was for your own good."

Through clenched teeth and barely audible she said, "I don't even know who you are. All of this time, I thought you were a farmer from a nearby village. I felt lucky that a woman my age, widowed, had a second chance to love and be loved by a decent man. Now I find out that you're a noble and a liar. Our life has been a lie." Tears began to fall down her cheeks as she spoke.

Setting his dinner aside, he approached her and put his hand upon her shoulder. She turned her face away and looked into the flames of the fire. He stood there with his hand upon her shoulder. He understood. He recognized fear, and Dandy was afraid. "Our love is not a lie. Our love is real. I may not be the farmer you thought I was, but I'm the man who loves you and always will." Taking her gently by the shoulders, he pulled her up to standing and embraced her as she wept.

After some time, he apologized, saying, "I must go and stand watch tonight, in case anyone decides to sneak off to the castle and tell King Traintor that I'm alive. I will be back as soon as I think it's safe and tell you more."

Knowing how feisty his wife could be, he knew he was pushing it to try and kiss her, but he also knew that anything could happen and he didn't want to leave it this way between them. Taking a deep breath, he took her face in both hands, looked into her green eyes, and kissed her upon the forehead. "I love you," were his parting words as he took up his farmer's axe and knife and went out into the cold night.

Dandy sat down near the fire, picked up her mending, said a silent prayer for his safe return in the morning, and carried on almost like she were in a trance. After all, what else could she do?

15

Mildrea was grabbed and dragged out of bed by some of Madam's servants. Madam was standing there, looking down upon her with pure hatred in her eyes.

"How dare you. I've given you everything, and this is your thanks? I had thought that you were different from the others. Different from these useless creatures." She waved a hand toward all the scarred women who had just pulled her out of bed. "You're no different. You're worse, bringing a man in here to help you escape."

Mildrea was confused and said, "I've no idea what you're talking about. What do you mean?"

This was met with a backhand from Madam. At first she didn't realize what had happened, but when the blood began to run warmly down her cheek and then drip onto the floor, she reached up to feel her face. Madam's sharp ring sparkled beneath the new blood that was upon it, and Mildrea realized she would now have a matching scar to the others. They all looked away from her, in shame or solidarity, she couldn't tell. She felt her chance of ever escaping was now hopeless, and she didn't care at all if she died right this very moment.

For the next two days, Creavy tried to beat the truth out of her. He tortured her by attaching giant iron clasps to her breasts and causing extreme pain until she would pass out. No matter how many times she told him she didn't know what he was talking about, he would not believe her. Madam came by a few times to watch and would leave after spitting on the ground at her feet. It was unbelievable, but these people who had kidnapped her and forced her into prostitution thought she owed them gratitude for looking after her and seemed genuinely appalled she could ever want to be away from them. These sadistic, horrible, abusive people almost appeared to enjoy torturing her.

After a time, Mildrea discovered the body's pain receptors shut down. Nothing Creavy did to her could hurt her any longer. She stopped crying out in pain. She stopped denying their accusations. She no longer tried to defend herself or answer any of their questions. She just sat there, tied to her chair, with her head hanging down, numbly taking everything they did to her in a sort of dull existence. She wondered if she might already be dead.

When she thought it was all over, Creavy leaned in close to her ear and spoke through his rotten, putrid cabbage breath, "I know about Thomas. I know you two were planning an escape. I will kill him when I next see him. You will never see him again."

Hearing these words caused her swollen, bruised eyes to fill with tears, and she stifled a sob, knowing Creavy would happily kill an innocent man who had only shown her kindness. Feeling something again made her realize she was not dead. Fuck, she thought, as she lowered her head in anguish.

Once Creavy realized he was getting no information out of Rose and that the only way he had left to hurt her was to kill Thomas and bring her proof of the deed, he set off, bringing a group of mercenaries with him. He didn't think an extremely tall man would be difficult to find and knew people were more than happy to answer questions and turn others in as long as they were paid. Knowing Rose was completely weakened from her two days of torture, he had Madam's servants put her back in her bed. She would most likely die there, but if she was still alive when he returned, he could present her with a gift, something from the dead Thomas, before he fucked her into a coma. He relished the thought and nearly ejaculated inside his trousers just imagining how incredible it would feel to fuck her as she died of pain, both internally and externally. Yes, he would go from village to village until he found the prick who had dared to try and steal his Rose away from him.

Madam was frantic after the intrusion into her chambers. She felt even more paranoid than usual and sent a messenger to Hildebrand. She wasn't sure how to tell him what had happened without angering him, but she certainly needed to step up security around her door. He had always told her they couldn't attract any attention to the doorway, which was why he never put a soldier there to stand guard. Well, that wasn't working, and she needed more protection.

When Hildebrand received the message from Madam, explaining what had happened and demanding he come down and see her himself, he laughed. Who did this whore of a woman think she was, making demands of him? He thought it may be time to put someone else in charge of the Scented Bitch Tombs, as he liked to call the lower castle where Madam was. The other side he called the Bastard Tombs, and although he had a man seeing to the day-to-day activities, he was the one in charge of the young men and boys he kept entombed there for the pleasure of anyone who would pay. He, of course, did not pay for his frequent pleasures and cruelty.

16

Mildrea was in a daze, but she realized her wrists and ankles were no longer bound to a chair. She recognized the feel of her own rough linen sheets and knew she was in her bed. With great care, she rose from her bed and put on the dress Madam always insisted she wore when she visited her. She even piled her hair up onto her head. She wanted to be able to enter Madam's special chamber without arousing suspicion from anyone in the hallway, so she must do this right. She was weak and battered, but after splashing cold water onto her face, she knew she could do this one final thing before dying. In agony, she slowly hobbled down the dimly lit hallway and peered into the chamber. Seeing no one there, she entered and went straight to the drawer where Madam kept her pipe and filled it with the sickly sweet resin that was hidden in a red tin behind a large vase. She then gathered up all the money from another drawer and tucked it away behind a loose brick. She wrote a note saying where the money was hidden and slipped out into the hallway. Heading straight to the room of Misty, one of the newest, youngest girls to have been brought unwillingly into this life, she gently knocked on the door. The girl opened it just a little, and Mildrea could see one of the meaner clients sitting on the edge of Misty's bed. She slipped the note into her hand, told her to guard it with her life until tomorrow, and then she leaned in and kissed her upon the cheek. It was the first time in four years Mildrea had purposely and willingly kissed anyone, and she hurried away as tears ran down her cheeks. Once back inside Madam's chamber, she took a sharp evil-looking serrated knife that Madam kept in the drawer where her cash had been, tucked it carefully into her bodice, and began smoking the pipe, settling herself down to await the evil woman.

Madam must've smelled her pipe because she came bursting into the room, yelling profanities. Her mouth fell agape when she spied Mildrea sitting upon her settee, smoking her pipe. She chuckled as she said, "Damn you, Rose, you've a nerve coming here, but you know I've always admired your spirit."

Mildrea patted the settee next to her, tilted her head to one side, and said, "Join me. I can make you feel better than you've ever felt before. You've taught me so well, let me show you what I mean."

Madam couldn't resist and sat down next to Mildrea, taking the pipe from her as she caressed her scabbing cheek. "I didn't want to scar you, but you must always remember who's in charge here. Now, you'll never forget. If you can continue to please me, I just may let you live on here with us."

Mildrea raised up Madam's skirt as she got on the floor in front of her. Just before she buried her face into Madam's squirming eager pussy, she said, "Oh I plan on pleasing you to death." She parted Madam's lips, causing her to moan and throw her head back. She then inserted what was at first pleasurable to Madam, and as she squirmed with delight, Mildrea thrust the knife deeper into her vagina. She kept pushing up until she was nearly up to her elbow. Madam screamed and writhed around, but Mildrea had her arm so far up inside the woman, there was no escape. The knife punctured Madam from the inside and poked out through her abdomen, shredding her from the inside out. They locked eyes as she withdrew her arm, leaving the knife and stood up to watch the filthy hag die a horrendous death.

"That's for all of us. I will see you in the afterlife, in the underworld, no doubt," Mildrea said, wiping her hand and arm on Madam's dress.

Taking one last gulping breath, Madam's head fell back. Mildrea pulled her skirt down and left her there, splayed and slaughtered on her settee. Then she walked down the hallway and out into the castle grounds, a free woman at last. She turned away from the brothel and headed for the main gates, hoping to exit the castle walls. Having had nothing to eat or drink for a few days, enduring horrendous torture, and smoking so much of Madam's resin meant she didn't make it far before she collapsed onto the earth. Just before she died, she saw her family before her. They were all saying goodbye and waving her off to find happiness for herself at the castle. Then, darkness was all around.

17

Madam wasn't found until the next morning, and even then, no one was in a hurry to deal with her body. The only person who seemed to have any sort of positive relationship with her was Creavy, and he hadn't been seen for a few days. Not since he'd tortured Rose and then gone off on a hunt for the intruder Thomas. Some of the servant girls drank the alcohol in her chamber while others smoked her pipe. No one was going to work on a day like this, and the entire place was filled with an eerie euphoria. Some women gathered up whatever few items they owned and left. They didn't know where they'd go, but they knew it would be better than this. They also felt a sense of urgency, as Creavy might return and get them working again.

Misty read the note and went into Madam's chamber to find the money Rose had left for her.

Women were passed out or extremely drunk or high throughout the room. They didn't seem to care that the body of Madam was sitting there with a torn up midsection and a pool of blood on the floor below. Misty acted like she wanted to join in the fun and waited until they were distracted for a moment to pull the stone away and grab the money. She quickly stuffed it into her bosom and started out the door. As she opened the castle door to the outside world, to freedom, she saw Creavy dismounting his horse. She ducked into the first room she could and listened for him to pass her by. The first place he would go would be Madam's office, and then when she wasn't there, he'd go into her chamber. She needed to move quickly if she wanted to get out of here alive. Especially if she was caught with all of Madam's money, as it would look like she had murdered the cretin. She had no idea where Rose was, but she hoped to find her and thank her on the outside of this prison.

Finding Thomas hadn't proved an easy task, so Creavy returned to the castle. There would be time, he told himself, to find and murder that man. He could wait, but if he wanted to be with Rose one last time before she died, he needed to return soon. He came in through a side entrance to the castle grounds and went straight to the brothel. He noticed a crowd of people, gathered about half a furlong away. They were looking at something then shuffling away. No doubt a dead animal or one of the beggar children who often froze to death in the night. He had more important matters to attend to and gave them little thought.

18

"Someone's daughter" a woman said, shuffling away and gesticulating in the direction of the young woman lying on the ground.

"What?" Waleda asked her, although she didn't really have to. There she was, motionless, peaceful at last. Could she be? Was it possible for someone so young? Perhaps she was only passed out or sleeping.

The silver-haired woman was reaching out to touch Mildrea, but Thomas placed his hand upon her arm and quietly said, "No, let her be."

It was then she noticed a crowd had gathered. But this wasn't right. Their faces weren't filled with sadness and shock as they should have been. Their faces were expressionless and uncaring. She looked up at him and then at all the people as he led her firmly yet gently away from the crowd. She allowed the man to lead her away through the bustling marketplace. Her feet were moving, but she didn't know where they were going, nor did she care.

Finally her feet would move no longer, and she looked at him and softly said, "Yes... she was." He leaned in to hear her, and she repeated, "Yes, yes she was."

"My lady?"

"She was my daughter, she was my daughter, she was my..."

The earth was spinning as her legs buckled beneath her. She wanted to be swallowed up. She no longer wanted to live. Her only desire was to join her child, wherever she was. The dirt tasted salty, and her eyes were stinging as she lay there sobbing. Then the blackness came.

Creavy was the only one who cried out in Madam's chambers. Not so much because she was dead but because all the money was gone. His first impulse, upon seeing her dead, was to rob her. Unfortunately for him, someone else had beaten him to it. He cursed and went straight to Rose's room. Discovering she wasn't there, he went all over the brothel, enraged and striking anyone who got in his way. Then he burst into the bright sunshine to search for Rose and the money. He started to get on his horse but then had a thought. What if the crowd was gathered around an injured or dead Rose? She might have the money on her person. If it was her, he could bring her back to the castle and search her body. He needed to see for himself.

As Creavy made his way into the throng of people milling about, he noticed a very tall man. It was the bastard Thomas who had beaten him up and then used his unconscious body to try and help Rose escape. Looking down, he saw that it was indeed Rose on the ground. Well, Thomas would keep for another day. Rose might have the money on her person, and right now that was a stronger pull for him.

Thomas looked up and saw that Creavy had lifted Mildrea up and was carrying her body towards the castle. There was nothing else he could do for her now. He lifted up the silver-haired woman and headed for his wagon. He needed to get home and to safety as quickly as possible.

After collecting her body and carrying her back into the castle bowels, Creavy laid Rose on her bed, ripped her dress off her, and began searching her everywhere. There were only so many places to hide money on oneself. Finding nothing, he searched the brothel frantically, and when it held no treasures either, he headed out, hell-bent on revenge with Thomas. Rose had been his steady earner and regular piece to do with as he liked. As far as he was concerned, Thomas was the only reason she was dead.

News got back to Hildebrand that he needed to find a replacement for Madam much sooner than he'd originally thought, as she had met a brutal death. He smiled as he thought things were turning out nicely. He decided to put an arrest warrant out on Creavy, for the murder of one Madam Shaska. Never mind that he didn't really think Creavy would've killed her, as he was one of the few people who actually seemed to like the old bird. Hildebrand, however, did not like Creavy and saw this as a way to tidy everything up to his satisfaction. Knowing he was a wanted man would at least keep Creavy away from the castle. A price was set on his head to be returned dead or alive, preferably dead, and orders were given to spread the word amongst the people, along with posters of Creavy's image. As soon as Jonesy heard, he went straight to the brothel to try and find his mate. Finding only a few drunken or drugged out women, he decided he might also lay low for a while and took leave of the castle grounds at first light.

19

Once outside the castle grounds, Waleda began to stir. Thomas found them a spot in the shade and leaned her sitting up against a tree. She was dazed and found it hard to focus and just stared at the grass. He offered her a drink of water, and when she refused to open her mouth, he gently tried pouring a bit upon her lips. This caused her to sputter and finally look at him.

"Milady, I need you to listen to me very carefully. We need to leave here, as soon as you feel you are able to. I have a wagon, well, more of a cart with goods, that you can ride upon, but we need to go soon. There is a terrible man, Creavy, who is looking for me. I believe he is the reason your daughter is dead. We must get away."

Waleda looked through him as he spoke, not hearing his words. She felt less alive than even a stone must feel and bent her head down to stare at the grass again.

Thomas looked around and decided they could no longer wait, as he knew Creavy would find them soon if they stayed. They needed to go now so he picked her up again. Her large, loose dress disguised how thin she must be beneath it. He hadn't realized how light she was when he first carried her away from Mildrea's body. She must be starving, he thought. He carried her to his cart and settled her down amongst his remaining goods. She put up no resistance at all, so he covered her up to both shield her from the elements and also to hide her from any of the king's spies who may be looking for them as they left town. He thought of Eleanor and wondered just what he would tell her about why he had stayed away from home for a few days and also why he was bringing this dirty, disheveled, seemingly mute, and starving woman home with him. Whatever he said, he knew Eleanor was kind and that her first reaction would be to care for this human. The truth of the horrors could be told later.

They rode on through the rest of the day and arrived at his home late into the night. Waleda hadn't spoken a word the entire time and put up no struggle as he carried her up the stairs and placed her upon a bed where she remained, still and lifeless, for the next few days.

When she awoke, she was lying in clean, crisp linen sheets, in a place unfamiliar to her. Her body and hair were clean for the first time in ages. She didn't know how much time had passed, nor did she care. Her entire body felt like a swollen sponge, heavy and full of something other than water. She was filled with emptiness. She knew the pain, anger, fear, and sadness were somewhere inside of her, but for now she wasn't able to find them. Motionless and silent, she closed her eyes. All she wanted to do was sleep. She didn't want to dream because the dreams were nothing but nightmares. She only wanted sleep.

Still unaware of how many days had passed, Waleda was in a dream state and lost in thoughts of better days past when someone entered her room. She opened her eyes to see a woman in her early thirties, looking upon her with kindness.

The woman smiled and then turned toward the door, saying, "Thomas, Thomas, she's awake, come, come!" Turning back to Waleda, she said, "You mustn't be frightened. My husband, Thomas, brought you to our house when you collapsed in the marketplace. My name is Eleanor, and I've been taking care of you."

She turned her face away and began to cry silently. She didn't understand who these people were nor why they were being so kind, and then remembering her daughter, dead upon the ground, she wished that she had been left to die also.

Thomas, the man from before, entered the room. He asked Eleanor to go and fetch some fresh water while he sat down on a chair.

When Eleanor had gone down the stairs, he said, "I understand you may not wish to speak to me. You must be in tremendous pain, but there is something I must tell you about the woman you saw in the marketplace. The dead woman... Your daughter."

She looked at him now and saw that his face was contorted with pain. Why should he care about her or her daughter? He didn't know them.

"Her name was Mildrea, wasn't it?" he asked.

At the mention of her daughter's name, she tried sitting up in bed but was too weak and lightheaded, so she remained lying there.

"That's it, isn't it?" he asked again.

"Yes" she managed to croak.

"Forgive me for speaking so freely, madam, but I feel you must know what happened to your daughter."

She said nothing to stop him, so he continued.

"Well, Mildrea, which is not the name she went by in the brothel where she worked. In the broth… there, she went by Rose."

Her tears came again. This time she could not control herself, and she let out a primal wail. Her daughter had left home for a better life, not to work in a brothel. The pain she felt for her was almost too much to bear. Then realizing that if this man knew her in the brothel, he must've been a customer. Finding an energy from deep within her pain and anger, she pulled herself off the bed, lunging at him and screaming that he was a foul, horrible man to have soiled her daughter like this. Thomas took her words and even the few pathetic punches she threw at his body and held her up as she collapsed into his arms, weak and heartbroken. He gently placed her onto the bed and stepped back.

"It's not what you think, but I think I'd better leave you to rest. My wife thinks I've just taken in a poor, starving woman, an old family friend whom I ran into. She knows nothing of your daughter yet. I'll return when you're feeling a bit better, and we can talk about her." Then he walked toward the door to leave. Turning, he said, "Just so you know, I never touched your daughter in any unholy way. Never." And with that, Thomas was gone.

Her husband died two winters ago, and now she was alone once again with dark thoughts of the nightmare that had been her life as her family collapsed around her. She returned to her numb silent state and just stared at the wall.

20

Bracknor kept watch all night, and no one left the village. He knew it was possible someone might wait until morning, when it would be less suspicious, but if that did happen, it would be several days before anyone could come after him, giving him plenty of time to get away. He decided to go home and rest a little, after he spoke with his wife. He hoped the night apart would've worked in his favor and that her anger would've subsided. It could, of course, always go the other way, and he might be met with flying crockery when he opened the door. Only one way to find out, but that didn't mean he had to make himself an easy target, so he headed around the side of his house instead of entering through the front door. He peeked through some cracks where a few stones had shifted. He knew he needed to fix them, but he did like having a way to peer both into and outside of his house without opening the front door. Besides, the gap was high up, so not easy for anyone else to notice or peek through. Even he, a tall man, had to step up onto a log to see into the hole.

Dandy was sitting in front of the fire, just where he'd left her. Her mending had settled onto her lap as she'd fallen asleep. The thought of waking her with a kiss and then settling into their bed was delicious, and just as he was about to climb down from his perch, he saw movement inside. Something was wrong. If someone was inside his house, why wasn't his wife awake? He stepped slowly down and stood just to the side of his door with his axe poised to strike whomever emerged from inside the house.

As the door opened, he was just about to bring the axe down when Dandy awoke and said, "Mariam, I didn't know you were in here. What brings you here so early today, and why didn't you wake me?"

Mariam chuckled, "I didn't want to wake you up, Dandy. I know how tired you must be, now that you're with child. I only brought by some fresh bread, as I baked extra. I also wanted to check on you, as I know last night must've been quite a shock. It certainly was to the rest of our village."

Bracknor didn't hear much beyond "with child." He was stunned. Why hadn't she told him? He didn't realize she could even have children. She was a childless widow when they met and had told him this right at the beginning in case it might make a difference to his marrying her or not. She said the fault must have been with her and not her husband. They both believed it to be true since they had a most active sex life and there had been no child before.

Things started making sense to Bracknor now. Dandy had been moving slower in the mornings for the past few months. She said she was alright, but he sensed she didn't feel completely like herself. She was also going to bed a bit earlier than usual, but he didn't complain about that, as he was more than happy to join her. He flung open the door and startled both women. Then he went to Dandy, knelt down, and promised he would take care of her always. Both her and their child. He kissed her hands. Mariam giggled and then discreetly left, closing the door behind her.

Dandy sighed and put her hand on his head. She so wanted to be cross with him, but she couldn't be. He loved her and she loved him. She lifted up his chin to look him in the eye. "Well, with a child coming into our world, Whistler—or Bracknor, or whatever the hell I'm meant to call you—I guess we really do need to dethrone the lying evil bastard sooner rather than later."

They kissed intensely, and then he said, "Let's just hope the others feel the same way."

21

Four years had taken their toll on the captive royal family. The king tried his best to remain calm and hopeful for his daughters, but the queen had gone into a deep depression and rose from her filthy pile of sleeping rags on the floor less and less each day.

Their youngest daughter, Genison, had succumbed to a terrible cough within the first six moons of their captivity. She brought up blood and hacked herself to death. It was a slow, painful death, and the king believed this was what started his wife on her road to madness.

Their eldest daughter, Alaria, cared for all of them: her father, mother, and sister, Soria. She befriended the guards, one in particular named Banton, and begged for extra scraps of food. She reasoned with him that King Traintor needn't know of Genison's death, so they should still have rations for five people. As the rations were disgusting and unpalatable to anyone who wasn't starving, the guard agreed to bring slop for five.

Their meager rations included water in a slimy bucket, which never seemed to get washed. If they were able to scoop the top layer and didn't disturb the deeper contents, they could drink it. That's as long as they didn't think of it too much. Closing their eyes was also the best way to eat the bowls of whatever meal they were given. At least that way they didn't see the bits of rats' tails, grubs, and other indiscriminate bones floating in the thick grey broth. Occasionally they put one in their mouth, but as long as they spat it out quickly, they might not vomit. Best to sip the broth from the side of the bowl, keeping their lips nearly completely closed to strain out the other floating, mostly unrecognizable, and sometimes living bits. As disgusting as it was, Alaria knew that, in order to survive, they must stay hydrated and fed.

One day, as she tried to get a few drops of water into the queen's mouth, her mother pushed her hand away and said, "Stop torturing me. I want to die and join my Genison."

It was the first thing she'd said in ages that made sense.

King Oshinor came to her side, cradled her in his arms, and pleaded with her, "My dear Elspeth, I know this life is atrocious, but we must be strong, for our daughters' sake. Bracknor must be coming for us. He simply must."

Elspeth gave him a blank stare then turned her face away. Frustrated and angry at their situation, he released her from his arms and moved across the room, shuffling his feet on the dusty floor. Elspeth rolled onto her side, her body facing the wall.

Alaria awoke before dawn and went to her mother to plead with her to drink. She reached out her hand and touched her shoulder. It wasn't unusual to be cold in their dungeon, but this was different. She pulled her hand back and then reached out again to turn her mother onto her back. She stroked her face gently before pulling a filthy blanket over her face and body, then she sat in the darkness and cried.

A few hours later, when Oshinor and Soria awoke, they all proceeded to lay Elspeth out as royally as they could. The king stared at his dead queen, disbelief painting his features. Soria sat off in a corner, crying and rocking back and forth.

When the guards came with their daily ration around midday, Alaria spoke quietly to Banton, and as darkness came upon them again, two men came into their dungeon and carried Elspeth away. Looking around, she knew if something didn't change, they would all die off one by one. Her father was weak and thin, his pallor slate grey. Her sister had begun mumbling and speaking words that made no sense to anyone.

Scratching out their days in the wall, she knew they'd been here for just over four winters, which meant she was seventeen years of age now. Although she hadn't been able to look after herself in this hellish environment, she believed she could use her youthfulness and sex to make things better for all three of them. She made a decision to survive. Knowing she couldn't share her plan with her father, as he would never agree to it, she set about mapping it out in her mind until she could next speak with Banton.

22

It seemed like days had gone by as Waleda still laid in bed, recovering and remembering her first few days on the run with Blythe and Kindness.

One morning, Eleanor entered with breakfast. "You should try to eat something now that you can sit up. It's been a few days, and I've only managed to get a little water onto your lips." She smiled, and Waleda felt grateful for her kindness. "I've brought you some fresh eggs from our hens. How does that sound?"

"Thank you. That sounds good," she said, shifting to a seated position in the bed.

Eleanor lifted a forkful of eggs to her mouth, but Waleda took the fork from her and motioned for her to set the tray down on her lap. For a moment, Eleanor watched Waleda eat, but as it became awkward for both of them, she got up to open the curtains and straighten up the bedding at the bottom of the bed. "I've washed and mended your dress as best I could, and if you feel up to it, you can come downstairs today and sit with me whilst I do my work. I even have some books to read, if you are a reader. Thomas is trying to teach me to read, but I always get the letters back to front and find it very difficult. Still, he has bought me some nice books."

"You have been very kind to me. I will come downstairs, and perhaps I can read to you, if I am still able to make out the words. My eyes don't see small things, such as words, as well as they once did, but I can try," she said.

Beaming, Eleanor said, "I would love that, but only if you feel up to it. You've done very well and eaten up all of your breakfast. Let me take your tray. Would you like any help getting dressed?"

"No, I'm sure I will be fine. I'll be down in a bit. Thank you."

After Eleanor left the room, Waleda felt a sadness in thinking of Mildrea and what she might have been like if she had married a decent man like Thomas. But was Thomas a decent man? She certainly had a few questions for Eleanor to find out more about her husband.

By the time she had dressed and walked down the stairs, the house was quiet and empty of anyone.

It gave her a chance to look around a bit. It was a simple, yet clean house. One she would have loved to have lived in. Her house on the farm had dirt floors with some slate near the fireplace, but this was a raised house with slats of wooden floorboards.

There was a decent sized room with a fire at one end, for cooking and heating the house, and a table with benches. There was another smaller fire opposite the first, with two chairs and a small table placed between them, making an inviting sitting area. It was something she had always wanted, but Blythe would say they weren't fancy people and could just as well pull one of their benches from the table to sit nearer to the fire if that's what they chose to do.

This house also had much more space than Waleda's did. Blythe and Waleda had a bed in one corner and a ladder that led to Mildrea's and Farnsly's beds above theirs. This house had an upstairs. It was Waleda's once-upon-a-time dream home. She smiled as she imagined her family here, then her smile faded as she grew sad. She was the only one left now, and here she was staying with complete strangers. They were kind, but they were strangers nonetheless.

Not wishing to take their kindness for granted, she looked around for something to do. Noticing a half-plucked pheasant on the table, she picked it up to complete the task. She was almost finished with the plucking when Thomas entered from a door at the back of the house. Eleanor's voice drifted in from outside also.

"Hello, I didn't mean to startle you, my lady," Thomas said.

"My name is Waleda, but you may already know that," she said, noticing her tone wasn't very warm. "Do you have time to tell me how you knew my daughter from a brothel and yet you didn't have your way with her?" She glared at him, waiting for an answer.

"Eleanor will be returning from the hen house in just a moment, but I will tell you everything tonight, I give you my word." And with that, he left by the back door, just as his wife came in through the front.

"I'm so glad to see you up. Oh, you finished plucking my pheasant. That is so kind of you, but you needn't do things like that. We are to look after you. A proper guest, my Thomas says."

"Well then, you should know that my name is Waleda and I appreciate your hospitality. I don't like doing nothing, and if it pleases you, the mistress of this house, I would like to assist you with your other chores."

Eleanor's eyes lit up, and musical laughter escaped from her. "Yes, Thomas said you were special, and I'm beginning to see it myself now that you are awake."

They spent the rest of the morning working side by side, preparing dinner and cleaning the house. When Eleanor sat down to do some mending, Waleda looked through the books and chose one with the largest print. Situating herself in a sunny corner to take advantage of the brightest light, she was able to read. It was a pleasant way to spend a day. She could not remember the last time she had the chance to relax and simply be.

For as long as she could remember, she had been working, as a wife, a mother, and then as someone on the run, trying to stay one step ahead and find her next meal. When she was a child, her grandfather taught her to read, and she taught both of her children. Farnsly took to it and enjoyed it, but his sister didn't see the point in it. "Why should I read about people who live wonderful lives when I shan't ever have that chance?" she asked.

Her grandfather was also the one to teach her to fish. He was very patient with her, as she preferred to let the fish swim away instead of pulling them out of the water.

She knew he was disappointed when she married Blythe. He wanted her to be happy and knew that she loved him, but he also knew that by her marrying a farmer, her life would be much different than it could've been had she married someone of her father's choosing.

Blythe used to say to her, "I know you married beneath you, Waleda, but I will do everything in my power to make your life the best life." He was a hard worker, and he stuck to his word. She never regretted marrying him. Being in this house, seeing how she could've lived, did make her sad though.

"Are you well?" Eleanor's expression was one of concern.

She realized she had stopped reading and was lost in her thoughts. "Yes, just daydreaming. I wonder if I might go upstairs and lie down for a spell. I'm feeling a bit tired."

"Yes, of course. Oh, I hope I haven't worn you out today. Thomas and I hoped you'd eat at our table for supper tonight."

"I'm sure I'll be alright by then. I just need a little rest."

After supper, Thomas told them how he met Mildrea, whom others called Rose. He talked of their friendship and the letter he had taken to the village, meant for Waleda and Blythe. He spoke of the hold

Madam and Creavy had over her and how one day Mildrea was no longer around. He explained how he had tried to rescue her. He would always regret his failed attempt and wondered what happened to her after that event. Both women were stunned listening to him. Although he had already told Waleda that her daughter was a prostitute, she hoped he had been mistaken. Now it seemed he spoke the truth.

"I am very tired. I think I'll go upstairs now. Thank you both for supper, and I'm sorry that I will not be helping you clear up everything, but I must lie down now."

Eleanor, clearly in shock as well, stood up to help Waleda. Taking her by the arm, she said, "Don't you worry about clearing up. Would you like me to help you to bed?"

Waleda feared that, if she spoke, she would break down and may not be able to contain herself, so she shook her head and made her way up the stairs alone, holding onto the railing with each step for support. Her legs wanted to buckle beneath her, and her heart was raw, pounding outside of her chest, exposed and crucified, yet somehow she made it to the bed and crawled under the covers, still wearing her clothing. Pulling a pillow over her head to muffle her pain, she released a torrent of pent-up frustration, sadness, complete devastation, and fury.

Morning arrived, and she didn't know if she had slept or not. She was once again numb. Alive, yet feeling dead. Since Blythe and Healer died, it had been her quest to find Mildrea. To find her and somehow make a life for them both together. Now she had no purpose. She had no one and nothing to live for. She made a decision that the only thing she wanted now was to find those responsible for all the pain her daughter suffered and make them pay. She would need to grow physically stronger, so she would stay with these kind strangers a bit longer. This way, she could glean more information from Thomas.

From the weather, she made it to be late spring. If she stayed here for another few moons or more, she may be able to convince Thomas to take her with him on one of his trips to the castle. She'd make herself useful and not let either Eleanor or Thomas know her plans, as she did not believe she'd return. Most likely, she would die trying to avenge her daughter's death, and she was prepared to do that.

23

Since all of them had been born into royalty, they never understood dealing with day-to-day mundane tasks, such as discarding and cleaning out their daily ablution buckets. An attendant in the castle always took care of those things. Since being imprisoned, however, it was left up to them. After a few days of all five family members sharing the same bucket, they realized no one would be dealing with it and asked their guards to allow one of them to do so. Alaria took it upon herself. It was definitely unpleasant, but in time, she appreciated the chance to walk outside of their cell to an outside pit where all manner of slop was either burned, buried, or fed to the pigs. It gave her a bit of outdoor air, which was most welcome from the dark cell she shared with her family.

About a week after her mother had died was the first time Alaria left their prison without the bucket.

Her father was stunned when guards came to escort her away. Having no idea where they were taking her, he began to protest and demand they take him instead.

Alaria looked at her father and said, "No, Father, I asked to go out. Do not worry. I will be back in a while, and things will be better from now on." Then she stood up straight and walked out with the guards, not looking back at her father lest she cry.

There was nothing else to do but hold Soria to his chest. The king died a little more. He was defeated. This was the lowest he had felt, as he could no longer take care of his own daughter. He wept into Soria's hair.

Alaria had worked out a deal with Banton. He could sell her to whomever he wanted to. There would be a daily limit of three men, and she'd have two days off a week to spend with her father and sister. He would keep the gold and share with her a few trinkets from the profit, but more than that, her family would be moved to a room with windows, clean bedding and clothes, a way to clean themselves regularly, and palatable food and water. The guard was a little surprised when the princess approached him with the idea. He looked her filthy body up and down, but thought if cleaned up a bit, she would attract men with more money. He could easily sell her in this condition also, but if he kept a better clientele, she would fetch more and last longer. He also knew the first buyer would be paying the most for unspoiled goods, from a princess no less, and would set out in search of the highest bidder.

Banton held no love for King Traintor and no ill will toward Oshinor. He had even worked for Bracknor as one of the former king's protectors. Once he learned Bracknor had fled the castle, he threw his sword into the ring for Traintor. He wanted to be on the side that paid, and at this point, that was Traintor. As far as he was concerned, he would make as much money off the current king, and should things change politically, he would go with the flow.

First things first, get her cleaned up. He hired some women to scrub her clean, cut the mats out of her hair, and put her in a fresh dress. She was a little too thin, but if she wore a loose dress, that wouldn't be so obvious. Besides, he knew there was only one part of her body of interest to most men, and it had nothing to do with the meat on her bones. She was barely recognizable after she had been bathed and freshened up and would bring him even more money than he'd originally hoped for. Perhaps he would be her first suitor. Reminding himself he could take his pleasure with her whenever he liked, he dismissed that idea and returned to his search for finding the man willing to pay the most for the virgin Princess Alaria of Welexia.

He had to be careful though because, if Hildebrand learned Banton was going into business selling the Princess Alaria, he would cut Banton out and take all profits for himself. After all, everyone knew Hildebrand made some of his money as an accountant, but it was the exploitation of the imprisoned young women and men that brought him most of his riches. And he'd never been one to take a competitor lightly.

Alaria returned to her family, who had been moved into their new accommodation. They were still prisoners, yet it felt a little less like it now. When she entered the room and saw her father and sister bathed and dressed in clean clothing, she knew she was doing the right thing. How else could they survive? She suspected that, before long, she would have been whored out anyway, and for nothing that would benefit her or her family. At least this way, she had some control over things. If ever she faltered, it's what she told herself.

King Oshinor found it difficult to look at Alaria when she returned. He was not a foolish man and knew there could be only one reason they'd had a change in their miserable conditions as prisoners. He was sickened that it had come to this. He watched his beautiful daughter move around the room with grace. She was fussing over Soria and offering to plait her hair for her. Both princesses had lost a considerable length of hair when the most ratty bits had been cut out, but it was still brushing their shoulders.

Soria loved the attention she was getting from her sister and sat there, feeling the gentle pull on her hair, not understanding why this change had happened to them but sensing a delicate situation. She could see Alaria was putting on a brave face, but their father seemed on the verge of either tears or an explosive rage. He walked around their new quarters, always focusing his attention out the window, like a caged beast ready to pounce. When she'd asked him about Alaria earlier and where they had taken her, he had simply shushed her and brushed her tangles away from her filthy face. She thought he would run to her and embrace her upon her return, just as she had done, but he stayed back and continued pacing and looking out the window.

Once Soria's hair was newly coiffed, Alaria kissed her sister on both cheeks and approached their father with great care. He was still facing away from her but spoke when she put her hand on his arm.

"I'm glad you have returned. I only hope this is a wise choice that you've made."

On the verge of tears, Alaria answered, "I didn't see any other way, Father. I love you and Soria. Please don't be angry with me."

Turning to face her and with tears in his eyes, he said, "Angry? How could I be angry with you? It is myself that I find abysmal. I wasn't able to keep my daughter and wife alive. I am the reason we are in this terrible mess. I didn't listen to my closest advisor, Bracknor, when he told me trouble was brewing. I naively believed our kingdom was happy." He collapsed onto his knees and wept.

Soria joined them, and they held onto one another and cried. As accomplished and brave as Alaria was feeling about the deal she had made, she prayed Banton wouldn't find her first client soon and therefore not return for many days. She wanted to live in their newfound luxury for a while before she felt soiled and ashamed.

24

Being a tyrant brought Traintor a sense of joy for only so long. He was bored with his position as king. There were too many people wanting so much from him, all of the time. He thought being on top of the kingdom, so to speak, would mean he was content. The truth was he was a miserable human and only found joy when making others miserable also. There were those who thought he was incredible because of the horrible ways he treated people, and they were happy about it. Since they were happy, it meant he wasn't making them miserable, and if they weren't miserable, he was finding no joy. He wanted everyone to hate him, then he could go on treating them all like shite and perhaps enjoy himself a little.

He would feign interest in someone one day and they'd savor the attention. The next day he would order them tortured for the sheer fun of it. Instead of this upsetting his followers, they found it exciting and relished in it with him. It did keep them on their toes, however, as they didn't want to be the next person to anger him and become his next victim. It was fine if it happened to those around them, though. With that, they had no problem.

He had never been content, and now was no different. He would say one thing to his followers, send them out into the kingdom to share the news, and by the time they returned within a day or two, he was saying something different. If they challenged him on it, he would have them tortured and then hung up for all to see as an example. Over time, people learned to never question his authority. They would go along with it, pretending he had never said the exact opposite. Many of his followers, especially those in the outlying villages, still thought he was an incredible leader. Those who felt otherwise kept their opinions to themselves because there were spies amongst their close friends and family. One didn't really know whom to trust.

It was just like the end of King Oshinor's reign, when man was pitted against man. King Traintor was supposed to make things better for everyone. He did make them better for the wealthy and elite, but for the common man, things were more difficult now than they'd been for years. Whenever they felt disillusioned with King Traintor, they would blame King Oshinor for running off and leaving them. He was easy to blame, as he couldn't defend himself.

One former guard, fleeing for his life, left the castle in the dark of night. Once far enough away from the castle, he began telling people King Oshinor had not run off after all. He and his family were imprisoned inside the castle dungeon by order of King Traintor. As far as he knew, they were still alive, but since they had received such ill treatment, they may have perished by now. Many villagers thought he was only trying to stir up trouble, just to find out who was for and who was against their king, so those who hoped it was truth, and not mere fantasy, mostly kept their enthusiasm to themselves. However, even with their doubts, a seed had been planted, and soon the seed grew roots that spread to the outlying villages.

25

The meeting the villagers held the night after Bracknor revealed his true identity had gone nowhere, but at least no one had left the village and turned him in either. He would talk a bit about this and that daily, trying to educate the villagers about how things worked in the castle. As he worked alongside the men, he could feel some of them turning their opinions his way and felt confident they would even follow him into the castle to rescue their true king. He acted with caution though, as he didn't want to scare anyone off.

Word of the king's supposed imprisonment reached as far as Bracknor's village one day, and this gave him the hope and courage he needed to act. He decided to use the upcoming village meeting to make an announcement. He spoke with Dandy about it beforehand this time, as he didn't want to embarrass or anger her again. He didn't want to do anything to cause upset, especially now their family was growing within her. Once he'd learned she was pregnant, he considered saying his goodbyes to his friend Oshinor and living out his days as a simple farmer, spouse, and father. He told himself it would work out, but day after day, he knew he was lying to himself. Dandy told him that even she knew him well enough to know he would never be content if he didn't at least try to rescue the true king. She also said he would know when the time was right.

Hearing their king was alive made him believe the time was now. He needed to act quickly before Newark realized the rumor about Oshinor being alive was spreading. It might give him reason to kill the true king and his family. He would show no mercy towards them. But why had he kept them alive these four winters? What reason could Newark have for doing so? Perhaps he got some sort of sick thrill just knowing the man he had overthrown was living in squalor beneath him day after day. Newark was one sick bastard and had a heart of stone, so that made sense in a twisted and perverted sort of way. Or perhaps he was keeping them alive as some sort of bargaining chip for his own escape should he be discovered as nothing more than a charlatan.

SOMEONE'S DAUGHTER

As the tired villagers shuffled into the meeting hall after a long arduous day of working the land, Bracknor could sense a mixture of moods. Some wished to be home, eating in front of their own hearth, resting their weary bones, whilst others were keen to hear what he had to say. His supporters seemed eager for him to begin. Some of them had been secretly itching for anything to change up their tedious lifestyle, even if it meant endangering them and their families. A silence fell over the room once all were in place. Dandy stood proudly with the women in the back, no shame or uncertainty upon her face this time.

Once the simple things were out of the way, Bracknor was called upon by the eldest man in the village, Manteith, who always led these meetings. "I know we are all interested in hearing what Whistler has to say this evening. Let's get on with it so we can return to our homes."

This was Manteith's not-so-subtle way of telling him to keep it short. He was, after all, an old man and grew more weary with each passing day.

The silence was punctuated by the occasional creaking of wooden benches, throat clearing, and a gentle shuffling of feet upon the stone floor. They were all attentive, and Bracknor proceeded, choosing his words with care, as he knew this may be his only chance.

Clearing his throat, he began, "I know we've all been hearing the rumors about King Oshinor." Upon speaking the name aloud, there was an intake of breath and gasps from many. He continued, "I trust all of you with my life, which is why I believe I am safe mentioning his name. These rumors, if true, mean there is no better time to attack the castle than now." There was an immediate uproar from the villagers.

"Attack? We cannot attack."

"They will kill all of us just for having this meeting."

"You should be ashamed of yourself, bringing this scourge upon our peaceful village."

"Go back to where you came from."

Some villagers stood and hurried out. One spat on the floor in front of Dandy as they passed her by. Manteith banged a wooden club upon a table, calling for order, and once the frightened ones had gone, he asked that there be no more outbursts.

"We should listen to everything he has to say, and he should be quick about it, before we make any decisions," he said, looking under his bushy brows at Bracknor and nodding, encouraging him to continue.

"Thank you, sir. I will keep it brief. Now, before I begin again, I ask that anyone remaining who feels uncomfortable with what I may say please leave now. There is no shame in leaving. I also understand that, if you stay, you are only listening. It doesn't mean you will agree with my plan."

People shifted in their seats, but all remained.

Bracknor added, "Since the village hall is no longer full, would it please Manteith if the women remaining were allowed to sit down. Some of them may be tired, what with working the land and… also they may be with child…"

He knew he was pushing it with Manteith, but he thought the women were more likely to listen and be supportive if they felt included in everything. Manteith gestured for the women to come forward and sit. They were surprised. They'd never been invited to sit down in a meeting with the men before, but they hurried forward.

Once all were settled, Bracknor began again, "Right then. Thank you for staying. I believe the time to attack the castle is now. I know how to get us in, as I lived there for many years. I also know where the dungeons are, and we could begin there, in search of our true king, King Oshinor. If we find him, we can help him and his family escape and then, when the time is right, present him to the people of the land, and they will see that King Traintor has been deceiving them this entire time. However, if King Oshinor and his family are no longer alive..." He hung his head low as he said, "If they are no longer alive, we will need to rush King Traintor and round up his men in order to form a coup, a takeover of the castle, until we can find a suitable ruler."

Murmurs scurried around the room as the villagers were discussing whether or not this plan would work or if it was pure suicide on their part. Bracknor let them settle before continuing.

"Now, I do not think we should go straight to the castle from here. I think we should head out of our village with the purpose of finding supporters in nearby villages along the way. I know there are others who feel exactly as we do. They will have heard the rumors by now, so our arrival won't come as a complete surprise."

One of the men said, "If our numbers grow, won't word of us get to the castle before we do?"

This unleashed a torrent.

"What are we expected to do when our menfolk are all gone? We can barely keep up with the work we are meant to do now."

"I think it's a ridiculous plan. Breaking into a castle. Pshaw!"

"We still don't know if you are who you say you are. Why should we follow you anywhere?"

Bracknor let them speak and waited until they paused. "Of course, it will not be easy. I understand your concerns and fear. These kinds of things are never easy, nor are they without risk, but I want my child to grow up in a different time than the one we are living in."

All of the women turned to look at Dandy when Bracknor said this. She looked only at him and smiled.

He continued, "If we allow King Traintor to continue his rule, our taxes will be raised more and more until we are quite literally starving."

There was silence for a moment until Manteith broke their thoughts. "If I was a younger man, I would join all of you in this struggle. I have observed Whistler... Bracknor, during his time living with us. I believe him. I also know how life has changed since King Traintor has sat upon the throne, and I've always been suspicious as to how he got there. We can work out a way for those remaining to help one another out with the necessary work so that no one feels overwhelmed. We elders are still capable of many tasks, and although we have been enjoying our relaxing years, we can muck in during times like this. I say we should vote on this and then proceed based upon the outcome of our vote. I know many walked out tonight, but I think we still have enough left in this room for a majority, should that be the way we choose. All in favor of devising a plan with Bracknor and then undertaking that plan, please indicate your response with a raised hand."

Nearly every one of the men raised their hands. Dandy was so excited, she raised hers also and then, blushing, put it down as she remembered it was only the men who voted in such matters.

Manteith was most solemn when he said, "That is settled then. Tomorrow, after morning chores are done, the men will meet here to begin their strategy. I have an inkling that some who left tonight will be at that meeting as well. They were simply too frightened when you spoke King Oshinor's name." It was as if he was further testing them by saying the name aloud. This time, no one gasped or reacted.

Then he advised them to be careful with their words and with whomever they spoke with. This plan would best succeed with only the right amount of information being leaked to the other villages. Some secrecy must be kept in order for things to work.

Bracknor looked over at Manteith and nodded a thank you, thinking there was much more to this man than an elder farmer of a small village. Now was not the time to inquire, but he knew that he would do so soon. With that, everyone returned to their own homes, their thoughts a whirl of excitement, fear, and disbelief that this was happening, and yet also hopeful that it was.

26

Creavy was furious. When he came upon the first village, he saw a farmer returning home after a day working in the fields. The terrified farmer was surprised when Creavy jumped off his horse and shouted at him. Rage was spewing from him, and it took the farmer a while before he understood what he was being asked.

"Where is Thomas?" Creavy shouted.

"What's that you say?" asked the farmer.

"Thomas, a tall man, the 'eight of a 'orse's 'ead. 'e comes through 'ere, I know 'e does."

The farmer figured out who Creavy was shouting about, and hoping to make this angry man calm down, he said, "Yes, I know who you mean. He sells us goods every few weeks. Nice man, that." Instead of the reaction he hoped for, this seemed to make the incensed man even angrier.

Creavy seized him by his hair and threw him to the ground before kneeling down and punching him in the face. "Where is 'e? The bastard stole my money."

As blood spewed from his certainly broken nose, the farmer said, "He hasn't been here for a week. I don't know where he is. He should be coming back next week though."

Not really caring whether the man was hiding Thomas or telling the truth, Creavy carried on beating him because he had to take his wrath out on someone. He had no money, he had no Rose, and his business partner, Madam Shaska, was dead. Once he found Thomas, he planned on torturing him.

By this time, others came out of their homes and surrounded the poor farmer who was being beaten to death. No one tried to stop the blue-eyed man because they figured he worked for the king and, perhaps, had good reason to beat poor farmer Weston. Although deep down they knew this was not true.

Sensing their presence, Creavy stopped what he was doing and stood up. The crowd parted as he made his way back to his horse. Pulling himself up onto the horse's back he said, "If any of you knows where I can find Thomas the vendor, tell me now. Otherwise, if I don't find 'im, I'll be back. It might be you I talk to next time."

Then he rode away, gathering his thoughts together. He had a plan of sorts now. If he had no luck finding Thomas in the next few days, he knew he was expected back here in about a week. He could always return and wait for him. Preferring to find him sooner though, while his fury was on the surface, he headed for the next village.

When the villagers realized farmer Weston was dead, they departed and headed their separate ways. It would do none of them any good to talk about what they'd seen, to discuss why it may have happened, or even to tend to the broken body. Perhaps one of the elder women would come out under cover of darkness and at least move the body to the edge of town, downwind, so they wouldn't have to smell him decaying. If not, they would walk by him every day until an animal carried off what remained of him. They had done it before. They could do it again. Only one young woman remained and stared at the dead man. Misty couldn't quite believe what she had just witnessed. She held back in the crowd with her shawl nearly completely covering her face because she knew Creavy and didn't want him to recognize her.

The silence was broken by an elder gentleman who approached her and said, "You don't want to be hanging around here, miss. People will wonder if you have any connection to farmer Weston. They might be thinkin' you'd be someone to point the finger at if that evil man returns. Especially bein' that you're not from around here. You're not one of us."

The words broke the spell she was under, and she reminded herself she was on the run. She was the one with the money Creavy was after and must not draw attention to herself. No, she wouldn't try to find a bed for the night here. It was too close to the castle. Also, why would a young woman, dressed in peasant clothing, have the funds to pay for a room? With those thoughts, she began walking out of the village. She'd have to be more careful where she stopped and with whom she spoke. Her life depended on it.

She walked all through the night to the next village. She tried blending in with villagers going about their day, buying bits of food here and there, sleeping behind a house for a few hours when she was sure everyone had gone to bed, only to arise early in the morning and set off for the next village. She wasn't sure how many days she traveled like this, but she hadn't seen any signs of Creavy, so she must have covered some decent ground by now. Besides, her legs felt like heavy tree trunks that kept trying to root themselves to the ground, so she decided to stop and find out what this village was all about. People hadn't reacted much when she first arrived. They didn't have the same fear and paranoia she had experienced in some of the villages nearer to the castle.

Seeing a barn and hearing the dull thud of milk hitting a wooden pail, she carefully took out a few coins and stepped inside. The farmer was seated on the other side of the cow, so she couldn't see them, only their feet. "Excuse me, I don't mean to startle you, but would I be able to buy some of your fresh milk?"

The cow mooed. The farmer said nothing but kept on milking. Pthud, pthud, pthud.

Misty stood there silently. She understood these people may also be terrified of strangers, and after what she had witnessed with Creavy and seeing that no one offered to help the poor farmer who was beaten to death, she decided slow steady movements and quiet gentle words might be her best approach. Growing up on a farm herself, she knew how to get an animal to trust you. She would use the same tactics here. She began to speak in a low soothing voice to the cow instead of the human. "There, there, girl. Aren't you lovely? Such a beautiful girl. Look at those lashes! Bet you win over all of the bulls with those big brown eyes."

The milking stopped, and the stool scooted back away from the cow. When the farmer stood up and looked over the back of the cow, it was not what Misty expected. It was a woman with deep green eyes. The woman sized up this intruder and then spoke. "Milk you'll be wantin', is it? Perhaps some food as well? And if you don't mind me saying, a good wash wouldn't be out of the question. My cow is a bit more fragrant than you at the moment. Follow me."

Grateful that someone had spoken to her and relieved that it was a woman, even after her time with Madam Shaska, Misty followed the woman across the farmyard to a house.

The woman with the pail of milk stopped at the doorway, turned to Misty and said, "There is a tub out back. There should be some rainwater in the large tub also. I'll fetch some hot water from the fire and bring it round to you. Then you can strip off and bathe. We can wash your clothes and hang them up near the fire inside to dry. I'll find you something to wear for now, unless you happen to have a change of clothes in that bag you've been clinging to like it was the king's gold."

Misty stood there. Should she run away now? Should she do as the woman said? She was simply frozen to the spot. Absolutely terrified.

"Well, go on. I'll not bite. You're safe here, lass," the woman said, smiling. "The men are out working the fields, so you won't be risking your modesty. Go on then. I'll be out in a moment."

Misty found it hard to believe someone would show another human any kindness after her short but despicable time in the brothel. Then she thought of Rose. Rose had saved her. She decided to trust this woman, so she took a step, then another. Yes, she would trust for both her and for Rose.

Dandy was heating up the water and wondering where this young woman had come from and what her story was. She was definitely on the run. That much was clear. She was also clutching that bag so tightly she was surprised she hadn't been robbed. Perhaps she had been, and this was all that remained for her. Ah well, there would be time for questions later. She thought she'd do her best to settle this young stranger in, and then when her husband came home, they could decide together how best to proceed.

27

Nearly a month had gone by, and Waleda felt stronger than she had done in years. She had eaten well and gotten back into the habit of regular household chores, which strengthened her considerably. At first, Eleanor tried to stop her from doing so much, but then Waleda noticed her pallor had changed.

"Eleanor, are your seasons coming along regularly?"

Eleanor, often shy, bowed her head. "No, I have missed my last two. I believe I am with child."

Both women wept happy tears until Eleanor said, "Thomas and I have been trying for years, and each time I have gotten to be a few months along, something always happens. We have yet to be blessed."

"Well, that is that then. I insist on bearing the brunt of the chores. I was successful with both of my confinements, and I will be here to aid you along the way. I learned much from my time with Healer, and I know just which herbal teas I will have you drinking to keep that babe right where it needs to be to grow within you. We shall start now. Sit over there by the fire, and I will make a special brew just for you."

Waleda had grown quite fond of Eleanor, thinking of her as a daughter. There was an innocence and sweetness to her that made her seem younger than her years. Caring for her and taking care of the household brought some respite from thoughts of what Mildrea must have endured. It was temporary, however, as those troubling thoughts were always lurking just behind a thin, shadowy veil in her mind.

Stirring their supper, Waleda was in a daydream of happier days when her children were wee babes and when she had dreams of what may lay ahead for them. A snort from Thomas's horse brought her back to the present. He had returned from his day of work away from home. Earlier, she had settled Eleanor near the fire resting and noticed she was now dozing. Quietly she went outside to meet Thomas to tell him his wife had some news to share, but before she could speak, she saw distress upon his brow.

"Thomas, what is it? What has happened?"

"There are rumors, my lady, that King Oshinor and his family did not leave the castle, but that they are still there, being held as prisoners."

Waleda was speechless, in complete shock.

Thomas unbridled his horse, and they spoke no more about it as they headed to the door of the house.

She put her hand upon his arm and said, "I think it best not to share this awful and also wonderful news with Eleanor. Not just yet." She didn't say why she thought this, but she was concerned it would not sit well with Eleanor, who was already frightened with her pregnancy.

Thomas nodded in agreement. His wife was slowly waking up as they entered, and he went to her for an embrace.

During supper, Eleanor took Thomas's hand to tell him that they, with God's will, were to be parents. He kissed her with fervor and passion, not minding that Waleda was witness to his joy. His joy, however, was tinged with fear because of the times past and perhaps also for the future under a tyrant, such as King Traintor.

To ease the awkwardness of his affectionate public outburst, Waleda congratulated them both and offered to clear the table, suggesting Eleanor may wish to go to bed. "You need to rest up whenever you feel weary, and I am here to be sure you do so," she said.

Her reasons were partially selfish, as she wished to speak with Thomas about the rumors. She needed to know what was going on at the castle before going to vindicate her daughter's death. Her mind raced with thoughts about what Thomas had heard. Could it possibly be true? Had their king, their true king, been living all this time as a prisoner? As awful as the thought of him and his family imprisoned was, it gave her fresh hope. There had always been suspicion around Newark suddenly becoming king and Oshinor running off. It just didn't seem to fit the man who had been peacefully running their kingdom.

She knew that, in time, she must tell Thomas her intent to return to the castle. As she had yet to formulate her plan, she was happy to stay with Eleanor for a while, at least until the first season of carrying the babe had passed. It was the least she could do to repay the kindness shown to her. She also knew she must avenge the death of her daughter and felt renewed with this new knowledge of King Oshinor. As soon as Thomas came back downstairs, she would talk with him. Now all she needed to do was wait.

Thomas was deep in his own thoughts as he descended the stairs back to where he knew Waleda would be waiting to discuss what he had told her.

She leapt up from her chair by the fire. "Thomas, you do know what this means? If what you have heard is true, then surely there are others out there who feel the same about the imposter and would wish him to be removed so that our rightful king can resume his title. Do you not agree?"

Her hopefulness was contagious, and he found himself smiling when he answered her. "Yes, Waleda, I agree with what you have said. I need to find out more. Many nights have passed since I brought you here. You have regained much of your strength and been so helpful with my wife around our home. I ask that you continue on whilst I try to find out more. Will you promise to do that for me?"

"Yes, of course. You have saved my life and been so good to me, how can I do otherwise, Thomas? I will stay with Eleanor. Where do you plan to go to find out more information?"

"I will resume my regular rounds, asking questions as I do so, trying to find out whether anyone else has heard anything of King Oshinor and his family. I will not mention him by name, of course, but I will find my way. I am always careful, and knowing Creavy may still be looking for me, I must tread with care, as much as these enormous boots allow me to anyway."

28

Once the men in Vintnos had met to strategize, they decided sending out small groups to the surrounding villages was their best plan. They would get the word out and arrange to meet up on the next waning moon before proceeding to the castle. This way, they would have darkness on their side when they went in for their rescue mission. It was agreed to call it a rescue mission instead of an attack, as the language frightened the villagers less. Bracknor only hoped that word of a rescue wouldn't get back to Newark. He was sure that if the true royal family were still alive, this would be all the encouragement Newark needed to end their lives. The villagers were urged to be cautious and as secretive as possible, remaining vigilant at all times.

There was another plan, should they need to bring forward the rescue day, but it would only be done with Bracknor's authorization, and if he had a very good reason to do so. Although he had revealed his true identity to his own fellow villagers, it was decided to keep referring to him as Whistler with everyone else, for safety. They told nearby villages the rescue was being organized by one who had been close to the royal family, but they spared the details. This was just in case anyone succeeded in spying and revealing their plans. Bracknor wanted to keep all in Vintnos safe from an attack on him.

So far, they had done a tremendous job of sharing the plan with only those who needed to know the details. They had even managed to catch those few who tried to sneak off in the night for a reward. Once caught, they were put into a jail of sorts in Vintnos. During the day, they picked up the slack and helped out in the fields because of the farmers who were traveling to other villages, building their army. At night, they rested in their makeshift jail cell. They were promised they would be released and returned to their own villages when everything settled down. They were outnumbered and decently treated, so none of them complained too much. Manteith was put in charge of the jailed villagers, and he delegated things with a military precision and a rare cunning. Bracknor saw that he definitely knew what he was doing and was most impressed with this man whom he had previously thought a simple village elder. Indeed, both men had kept secrets. His own were now out in the open, but when would Manteith's secret emerge, he wondered.

Returning home at dusk, Bracknor put his horse in the barn for the night. He'd come from a meeting in the next village and was feeling more confident, as the army was growing. He wanted to take on Newark soon but felt the plan in place was the best one, so he needed to be patient. He paused outside of his home as he heard Dandy speak to someone else and waited until he heard a reply. When he heard a young woman's voice, he entered.

Dandy rose from her seat and crossed to kiss him on the cheek. "Hello, my love. You must be exhausted. You'll have noticed we have company. Whistler, this is Misty. Misty, my husband, Whistler."

Jumping up, knocking over the stool she sat upon in her haste, Misty blurted out, "Pleased to meet you, sir. Your wife has been most kind. She's taken wonderful care of me. I honestly thought that there was no kindness left in the world, seeing the things I've seen. I am grateful for everything."

When Bracknor said nothing, Misty uncomfortably went on.

"I... I... I will pay for the food." She quickly added, "I don't have much money, but I am happy to pay. Nothing comes free in this world. That's what my father always said." Upon mentioning her father, she trailed off and righted her stool before sitting down and looking into the fire.

Dandy looked at Bracknor, pleading with him to speak.

He cleared his throat and began, "Well, unless you've eaten a harvest season's worth of our food, I don't expect we will need payment. I know my wife is gracious, and if she's invited you into our home, I trust that she had good reason to do so."

Misty turned to look at him. There were tears trying their damndest to escape from her eyes. She didn't want to risk trying to speak and cry in front of these people, so she nodded her head in thanks to both him and Dandy.

After a moment, Bracknor spoke. "Well, I am quite hungry, my dear. Anything I can do to help with dinner?"

Dandy knew this was his way of letting her know it was okay that she had brought a stranger into their home. She breathed a sigh of relief. Now was a trying time, and people couldn't be trusted. But he had always told her she had a way about her when it came to seeing inside a person's soul, so he knew he could trust her about this young woman.

"No, Misty has been helping me with my chores today. Why don't you go get washed, and we will get dinner on the table." She kissed him on the cheek again as he headed outside to wash up. When he had gone out the door, Dandy crossed to Misty and hugged her. She didn't know what her story was, but she could tell it held a lot of darkness and pain.

Misty melted into her arms for the hug but was careful not to stay too long or she knew the tears would start. She stepped away and, trying to compose herself, said, "What would you like me to do, ma'am?"

29

Seven nights had passed, and still Banton had not returned to give Alaria any news about her first liaison. The atmosphere with her father had gotten a little better. Both of them tried to pretend that the inevitable would never happen. She found, if she was quiet, her father would also be this way. For their sake, she must be strong. If she could save her father and sister and prevent anything like this from ever happening to Soria, she would be happy. She noticed how some of the guards had taken to staring at her sister in lewd ways whenever they entered their prison chamber.

Soria, in her naivety, had even begun to flirt at times. She may be fifteen winters of age now, but being held in captivity since she was eleven meant she was very much an innocent child and had no idea what her flirting could cause for her. Whenever Alaria observed it, she would intervene with haste. Soria would sulk and ask why she never let her have any fun, but Alaria would smile and change the subject, often catching her father's eye as she did so.

Since all arrangements went through Banton, she told a guard she wished to speak with him. She wanted books and some art supplies so she could proceed with her sister's education whilst they were here. At least it might be a distraction for them. She noticed her father had begun pacing the perimeter of their room with much more regularity. If he could see his daughters living a near to normal life, it might help him also.

Banton arrived just as their evening meal had been taken away. He escorted Alaria outside of the prison chamber, as he didn't want to speak in front of her father. "Well, my princess, I have some momentous news. I have found you your very first suitor."

Upon hearing his words, her dinner came back up inside her throat, and she wondered if she might expel everything she had eaten. Swallowing it back down, she put on a brave face and asked, "Will you keep me in suspense? Might I be allowed to know the identity of him? Or at least his age. It might help me to prepare myself a little more to his liking."

She's plucky, this one, thought Banton. "Well, you see, princess, that is the tricky part. He is conducting his business through another, so I am unable to give you those specific details. I can, however, tell you this. He is to arrive thirteen nights from now. I thought it best to take care of business when the king was away visiting his most loyal supporters in their villages. The king leaves in ten nights, our visitor arrives in thirteen."

Reminding him she needed to remain healthy and hygienic in order to bring him the riches he desired from renting out her body, she asked for more garments. Simple dresses for the women and breeches and a shirt for their father, the king. He agreed a clean-smelling princess was more likely to attract higher paying clientele. Upon occasion, he had visited the Tombs himself and knew the women there bathed daily, even if their clients did not.

She also told him she must be allowed to empty and entirely swap out their daily bucket for a rinsed and dry one. She explained that with both her sister and her having their monthly flowers, this was now more necessary than ever. Banton had no problem discussing how he would sell Alaria's body out to strangers for a profit, or their daily shite, but as soon as she spoke of her menses, he became uncomfortable.

She pounced. "I've been having my menses since I was twelve years of age, and I've always used simple cloth for this. My servants made sure I had a continual supply, and I never really thought much about it. These past few years have been a bit more difficult."

"Alright, alright, no need for all of this talk," Banton said, shaking his head.

She continued, "What? You can go into battle, even kill a man, but you cannot handle me talking of my blood flow? I took my dead sister's undergarments so I could tear the fabric into smaller pieces. When my mother died, I asked Soria for assistance, as it was such an awful thing to do, to tear the clothing off of our dead mother's body. We told our father to look away, as we knew he would not understand why, but we knew it was a necessity. At first Soria's menses were delayed, most likely a result of our horrendous diet. Mine even became irregular and scant."

Banton was looking away now, disgusted. When she stopped talking, he looked her way.

She forced a smile when she said, "Now that you have us living in much better conditions, we are both flowing in sync with one another. It happens, you know, amongst women living together. A bucket for our daily ablutions and another to bathe ourselves and wash out our rags would be most welcome."

He nodded in agreement.

Walking back to her cell, all she could think of was that she still had more time until her first client. Yes, she still had more time.

Her thoughts were interrupted when Banton seemed to read them and said, "Course, when our high-paying chap has finished with you, I have several others lined up. I'm thoughtful though, they won't begin until the next day. I know, I know, only three a day with two days off. But the king will be gone for at least a fortnight, so I reckon that's maybe ten working days times three customers a day. Oh yes, princess, you will make me a very wealthy man, and for that I am grateful. So grateful. Once you've been soiled, you and I will get to know each other a little better as well. I am quite looking forward to that, I can tell you."

The corridor became even darker upon hearing these words.

He unlocked her door and winked when he said, "Have a good night, princess. Sweet dreams, maiden. I know what I'll be dreaming about."

Feeling as though she had been punched in the stomach, Alaria entered the room where her father and sister were awaiting her return. They were anxious, and although she tried to smile and act like everything was fine, her father knew something terrible must have happened. He tried to look her in the eye, but she avoided his gaze.

"I have just asked for some reading material and also some pigments to be brought to us. No need to let our minds deteriorate whilst we are in this situation. I believe that a young lady, such as yourself, Soria, should be schooled in the same ways that I have been, so I will take it upon my humble self to teach you whatever I am able to. We can always ask the elder gentleman we share our quarters with for his input." She smiled at her father as she spoke the last of these words.

Despite his misgivings, he smiled back at both of his daughters.

Banton was true to his word, and the things Alaria had requested were delivered to their chamber the next morning.

Soria was overcome with excitement and jumped up and down. Taking hold of Alaria, she kissed her on the cheek and said, "I do not know how you are able to make our lives better, sweet sister, but I do know that if I had to be held in captivity with anyone in the entire kingdom, I would choose you. You are the best big sister that ever there was."

"Alright, that is quite enough now. We will begin with our first lesson after we have eaten and cleared away our breakfast items. Perhaps you would like to explore the contents of our newest supplies and decide where you would like to begin on this educational journey. I need to speak with Father for a moment."

Soria squealed and skipped over to the box.

Alaria gently pulled her father aside. "Father, I overheard some of the guards talking when I was out in the corridor last night. I am not entirely sure what good the information will do for us, but I sense something in the air, and I wanted to speak with you about it."

Oshinor sighed with relief. He thought Alaria was going to tell him she would be spending less time with him and Soria. This could have only meant one thing. Instead she was sharing some news with him, so he waited for her to proceed.

"The guards were saying that Newark and his army will be visiting the villages soon. They will be gone from the castle for a fortnight or thereabout. Do you think we would be able to devise some sort of escape plan whilst they are gone? We would have to act quickly though, almost as soon as he leaves, to take advantage of the shifting of responsibility within the castle."

Her father just looked at her.

"Father, did you hear what I was saying? We might be able to escape."

"Yes, yes, I heard everything you said. It is just that I am amazed at how your mind works. We are held captive for four winters, and you seem to be the only one alert enough to potentially devise an escape plan. You are a credit to your mother. She always had the strategic mindset that I did not. She also insisted I keep Bracknor nearby, as he too was always looking one step ahead. Please, tell me what it is that I can do to help you."

Alaria's face fell. "Father, I may be a princess, but you are the king. I am looking to you for guidance. I have done my best to make our living conditions better, trying to keep us alive, but you are the one who must lead us now. Please, Father." She lowered her chin as tears of frustration and anger ran down her face.

The king reached out and took a hold of his daughter's face, lifting it so they were eye to eye. "Yes, my dearest. You are right, yet again. However, I do not wish to lead on my own. I wish for you to equally lead with me. If we manage to escape… When we manage to escape and take back our kingdom, I will share my crown with you, as you are the true leader of this family now."

"But, Father, you know that I may be a soiled princess by then. I am still chaste, but that is to change soon. This is the other reason I am set upon us escaping before that happens."

The king drew her closely to him for the warmest hug he had given her in four winters, possibly even her entire life. "Well, that gives me even more fire within my belly to succeed in escaping. I would say we should devise a plan, but knowing you, I believe you may already have one brewing in your beautiful mind. Am I correct?"

She smiled at him as he kissed her upon the forehead.

30

After dinner had been eaten and cleared away, Bracknor suggested they all sit and chat. He began by asking Misty where she came from and what brought her to their village. She had nothing to hide, apart from her embarrassment at having worked in the brothel at the castle, but she thought she could always say she worked as a kitchen maid. These people would not know. Apart from that, and the amount of money she had, she would tell them the truth as best as she could.

Her village was many weeks away, and she wasn't sure she could find her way home or even if she wanted to return there. One day, a group of men who worked for the king came to her village. They were seeking young women to work for the royal family. They promised it would be a better life than the one she had on the farm. Her family, nearly starving, felt they had no choice. She did not want to go. She was in love with a young man named Solem and hoped to become his wife and farm together. She had never been very close to her parents, and they told her it would be for the best. A sum was settled upon, and she was loaded into the wagon with a few other young women, already heading to the better life promised them.

As soon as they were out of the village, the team stopped and began to put ropes around the wrists of the women. Those who had just boarded the wagon were confused and started to protest. A harsh slap across the cheek silenced the loudest protestor. Whilst some men finished tying them up, a tall, thin man with icy blue eyes stepped forward. This was the same man who had bargained with her family. He seemed especially keen that she join the king's ladies and told her parents they were getting twice the amount as their neighbor was because their daughter was young and beautiful. He explained that the more attractive a woman was, the more likely she would get to work with the king's immediate family.

"Now, ladies, forget about your families. They 'ave already forgotten about you. They sold you. You now belong to me, Creavy. I am a fair boss but I 'ave been known to 'ave a 'ard 'and when it comes to discipline."

Here the men laughed at his words.

Creavy smiled at them before continuing. "Now, 'ere are the rules. I suggest you remember them. Outside of each village, we will stop and the rope that is keeping you safely within the wagon will be removed. When we get into the village, you are to speak to no one at all, not even each other." His voice barely above a whisper, he said, "Should you forget this important rule, you will be silenced, like your friend 'ere was, and then once far enough away from the village, so that no one will 'ear your screams, you will be tied up, whipped, and left to be picked apart by whatever creature, man or beast, finds you. 'ave I made myself clear?"

The only sound was whimpering from the terrified women.

"'ave I made myself clear?" Creavy shouted, which startled all of them into replying with muffled affirmations amidst their crying. Laughing to himself, he said, "That's good then. Let's be off."

Every day continued like this for the longest time. Misty said that although they were fed decent enough food, a few of the women became ill. Anyone who had a runny nose or coughed too often was taken away in the night and never returned.

One woman went mad, crying and muttering to herself. True to his word, Creavy had her removed, tied up in a splayed position, and ripped her clothes from her body, and the lashes began. At first she screamed, but then she fell silent. Her skin was raw and bleeding when Creavy had finished with her. He said something about stopping only because his shoulder and arm were sore from all the hard work. Then he told the men they needed to get back on the road.

Losing any of the women seemed to anger him because he would go on and on about how he'd paid good money for them and how now the rest of the women would have to work even harder when they arrived at the castle.

Misty fell silent for a few minutes, staring into the fire. She seemed to be somewhere else.

Dandy interjected, "You poor poor dear. I am so sorry. You need not continue."

Misty came back to them and said, "No, it feels good to tell someone my story. If it isn't too much for you, I'd like to go on."

Dandy nodded, so she continued, "I was very careful to turn away if anyone coughed or sniffled. My auntie, our village healer, had always said that the air of an ill person was infected and would spread to others. Of course, everyone in our village thought she was a bit mad, but I decided to take no chances.

We were road weary but our spirits rose when we saw the castle gates. We thought it would feel so good to get off of the bumpy wagon."

She wasn't clear how to continue here because she didn't want to let on about the brothel, but she looked at these people and realized they'd probably already guessed she wasn't going to be working for the king, so she continued.

"I'm not proud of this next bit, so I'll keep it simple, only saying what I think needs to be said for you to understand."

She went on to explain about Madam and the brothel beneath the castle. Her voice became almost monotone and quiet throughout all this. The short time she was working for Creavy and with Madam was awful, but there was one person who had been nice to her. A woman, a few years older than herself, named Rose.

Both Dandy and Bracknor noticed how she changed when telling them the next bit. She almost brightened up.

In the mornings when they were bathing, Rose smiled at her and tried to make her feel better about her surroundings and the life she now had. Just recently, there had been a frantic commotion in the brothel. An intruder had come in and tried to kidnap Rose. Everyone went into a frenzy, and the next few days were a bit chaotic, not the orderly regime that Madam usually kept. One day, Rose knocked on her door. She hardly recognized her, her face was so swollen and beaten, with a new scar running down her cheek. She handed her a note and told her to guard it with her life until the next day. Then she leaned in and kissed her gently on her cheek before walking away. Misty placed her hand on her face when she told them this, making it seem as though it was happening right now.

Dandy could barely contain herself, "So what did the note say?"

"Yes, sorry. It told me to go into Madam's secret chambers and where I would find my key to freedom. I looked where she said and found some money. So I took it and ran."

Unable to hold her pain in any longer, she broke down. The rest of the story came out between sobs as Dandy tried to comfort her. They learned she had seen Creavy beat a man to death about five or six days ago. He was furious and looking for someone named Thomas, a vendor. To her horror, no one intervened. They even left the dead man lying where he died. She only walked away when another villager told her not to hang about or she might be caught up in something. She had been on the run ever since, careful not to spend much money, lest anyone be suspicious.

"To be honest, I've never really had more than a few coins, so I have no idea how much she gave me."

Dandy looked at her with compassion then at Bracknor. He had been silent throughout Misty's story. He had known of the brothel on the castle grounds. He had tried to tell the king, but Oshinor wouldn't listen. He was pretty certain Hildebrand still had a hand in the pot, even if Misty hadn't mentioned him. He had heard of this Creavy fellow. A snake whose name seemed to crop up whenever something unsavory took place. It made perfect sense that he would be attached to Hildebrand somehow.

Then he had an idea. If this young woman, or girl more likely, had been at the castle within the past week, perhaps she could tell him some things that might be useful. He had been away for four winters and felt like a blind man leading his army in to rescue King Oshinor and his family. Anything at all she knew would help. Also, who was this Thomas the vendor, and why did Creavy want to find him so badly? He would put the word out about him as his men visited other villages. Perhaps Thomas could also keep him informed of a few things.

He asked Misty if she had heard any rumors that King Oshinor and his family were still at the castle. He kept it vague, as he wanted to hear what she knew, if anything, and not give her any ideas.

She shook her head and said, "The only thing I recently heard about the king—Traintor, not Oshinor—is that he and his entourage will be making a tour of the villages soon. In about another five or six days, I think. The customers at the brothel were excited because it meant that the king's army would be gone and they would have a better choice of which of us they wanted to take to bed. We were also glad because it meant we might not be so busy for a while. Breaks there were most welcome."

She shifted uneasily before saying, "If there is nothing else, sir, I would like to go to sleep soon. It has been a very long day, a very emotional evening, and I need to head out at first light. If you don't mind, I will bed down behind your home, same as I do in the other villages. Thank you for your kindness, miss. I didn't believe there was any left." With that she rose, felt her dress to see how it was drying, picked up her bag, grabbed her shawl, and headed for the door.

Bracknor was so embedded within his thoughts, he murmured an agreement of sorts.

Dandy jumped up and said, "Absolutely not. You will absolutely not sleep outside. You will sleep here by our fire. We can easily make up a pallet for you. Isn't that right, Whistler?"

This aroused Bracknor from his thoughts. "Pardon? Oh yes, yes, you must sleep in here, where it is safe and warm. I'm sorry, I had not realized what you were saying before. Please, accept our hospitality for the night."

"And tomorrow morning we will discuss what happens next. I am not happy about you traveling from village to village all alone. I may have need of help around here, especially as my husband is gone more often these days." Dandy shot Bracknor a look that let him know he had taken a misstep somewhere.

31

Everything was happening with haste, and now they must proceed with the alternate plan. It would be easy enough to get word of that out. The villagers had an autumnal celebration, which was considered pagan by King Traintor. As far as he was concerned, since he had taken over the crown, this ceremony was no longer taking place. Certainly in the villages nearest to the castle, they had not been able to observe it properly for the past four winters, but in the villages further away, such as Vintnos, not an autumnal season had gone by that it was not celebrated. It happened on the full moon, the harvest moon. The festivities would begin with an enormous bonfire being lit, burning an effigy of a spirit man made of trees and twigs. He was burnt to appease the goddess of the harvest so that she would bless them with an abundant crop and just the right amount of rainfall, not too much, not too little. This harvest celebration and its goddess might be just what he needed. He had an idea that he wished to run by Manteith first.

Once Misty was bedded down for the night, Bracknor told Dandy that he urgently needed to speak with the elder and to not wait up for him. He kissed her with vigor before heading quietly out the door. She knew to always bolt the door at night, especially when her husband was away, so she did that before lying down and praying that he would return to her soon. She could sense that something Misty told him had gotten him excited, and there was a discomfort in her stomach.

Gently stroking her abdomen, she whispered into the night, "There, there little one. Your father is trying to make things better for you and the life you will lead. Everything will be just fine. You will see." Then she closed her eyes and prayed some more.

The old man was just beginning to nod upon his bed when there was a faint knocking on his door. So faint that he thought he may have imagined it. Closing his eyes again, he heard tat-tat-tat. This time there was no mistaking. Who in the mother of celestial beings was knocking upon his door at this hour? he thought.

He slowly rose, picked up an axe, and put on his most feeble voice. "Hello, is someone there? It is very late, and I am a frail old man in need of rest on the remaining nights bestowed upon me."

"Manteith, it is I, Bracknor. I have news that will not wait until morning. Please speak with me."

Sounding twenty years younger, he said, "Alright, I will allow it." He had just gotten the door unlatched when Bracknor entered, closing it and latching it behind him.

"I have learned that King Traintor will be away from the castle, visiting his adoring followers. This would be the perfect time to attack... rescue, as he will take his army with him. He would never go anywhere without his army. Of course he will leave a few men behind, but these will not be his finest warriors," Bracknor blurted out.

"Slow down, Bracknor. Sit. I have never seen you this excited before. I will brew us up one of my nightly concoctions, quite potent they are too, and you will tell me your news again, this time including all of the details, such as where you learned of this."

Bracknor knew Manteith was as stubborn as he was old, so he realized he must do as he was told if he intended on getting anywhere with his plan. He sat down near the fire and waited for the concoction to be brewed. When the elder was ready to listen, he began again, this time including Misty in the story so Manteith could judge for himself the validity of the claim.

"Well, it does seem to be true then, does it not? Tell me, great strategist, how do you plan on using this newly learned information?" Taking a sip, the elder man leaned back in his chair, stroked his beard, and tilted his head to the side as he looked directly into Bracknor's eyes.

"We will have to use the alternate plan. If we wait until the waning moon, Newark may have returned to the castle. Yet, if I light the bonfire in four nights' time, we are still in a waxing moon and not a full moon and the other villagers will know we are to gather up and head out the next morning. We can be at the castle four days after that, which means Newark and his army will have two or three days of travel away from the castle already. It is the perfect time to storm in and rescue our King Oshinor and his family. Would you not agree?"

Hearing the words spoken aloud, even by himself, gave Bracknor a newfound hope. The words seemed to rekindle a spark that had been barely burning inside of him. Leaving his king, his best friend, was the hardest thing he had ever done, and now, knowing he may be given this one chance to rescue him left him breathless.

Again Manteith took a sip, tilted his head to the other side, leaned forward, and spoke. "Do you ever wonder who I am? Have you ever noticed anything about me that made you think I may not be the simple farmer, now an elder of course, that I appear to be? Ah, ah, ah, before you answer, Bracknor, hear me out."

Bracknor had anticipated this conversation taking place, but he wasn't sure this was the appropriate time, as there were other, life-saving plans to be getting on with. Still, if he had learned anything about Manteith in his time here, it was that the man was like a mountain and could not, would not move any faster than he deemed appropriate at any given time, so he took a deep breath and decided to simply listen to what was to be said.

He listened closely as Manteith revealed his true name to be Lexford. He was the youngest brother of Oshinor's father, meaning he was King Oshinor's uncle. He had intended to assist the young Oshinor, only thirteen years old, when his father died. They didn't have much time together, however, because Welexia and Restunia had been engaged in an ongoing feud for years, which turned into an out and out war. Lexford, as commander in the king's army, went away to fight in one of the bloodiest battles the Kingdom of Welexia had ever known.

Although Welexia succeeded in winning the battle and sending the other soldiers scampering off, he and many others were taken prisoner by a band of outsiders, fighting under a rebel flag but loyal to the enemy king. They were taken aboard a ship and sailed to neighboring Restunia. He was imprisoned with the other soldiers and ordered to serve hard labor. Many of his fellow prisoners died of starvation and overwork. He was determined to avoid this destiny, and after plotting and planning, he escaped. After many days on the run in a land he did not know, he made his way back to Welexia by earning his passage on a ship through exhausting work.

By the time he returned home, he was a broken man and did not feel like royalty anymore. Would he even be welcomed at the castle? The young Oshinor must have been overwhelmed ruling a kingdom in such difficult times. He felt guilty for leaving his nephew all alone, so he decided to hide his identity and settle down in a small village, called Vintnos, far away from the kingdom's capital. Over the years, he heard mutterings about the Earl of Newark, and then when Oshinor was overthrown, presumed dead, he decided to continue living life as old farmer Manteith, the guilt gnawing away at him even more.

Smiling and shaking his head, Bracknor leaned back and chuckled to himself. "I must say, I was not sure exactly what I was expecting you to say, sir, but I do know that it certainly was not this. I am humbled. How in the seven kingdoms have you managed to keep your identity a secret all of these years? It truly is incredible. You telling me this, and with the news that Misty shared, I think I absolutely must put more stock into rumors when I hear them."

He went on to explain that, as a child, he remembered the great Commander Lexford. He also remembered those who returned from the triumphant yet fierce battle, only to be told Lexford had been killed on the battlefield. They had no reason to doubt this, as the stories of the gruesome battle were relayed for years. Songs had been written about Lexford and his men. King Oshinor mourned his uncle's loss for months. Bracknor knew he had put on a brave face, but it had taken a huge portion of his heart, losing both his uncle and his father in such a short period of time.

Manteith shook his head. "Well, at least with my nephew believing I had died, he would not have felt I abandoned him purposefully. My heart breaks for his sadness, and I do not know whether I will ever be welcomed back as family, but…" He swallowed the lump in his throat and wiped tears away from his eyes.

The men sat in silence whilst the elder composed his emotions.

Finally he cleared his throat and spoke. "We've more important things to be concerned with for now. Seems like you are not the only one to keep your true identity a secret. From the day you arrived, I suspected there was more to you than a simple farmer as well, Bracknor. I believed the time would one day come when you shared your identity with me. That time came. Now, we have much work to do. Between you and I and our knowledge of the castle, we should be able to devise quite a plan, would you not agree?"

Bracknor smiled as he knew Manteith was toying with him by using the same words he himself had used. "I agree… sir? Or is it m'lord? Commander? How would you like me to address you?"

"Please address me as you have always done, showing me the respect you have given to me as an elder of this village. No one else need know our secret." Then he added with a wink, "At least not at this time."

32

It was early morning, and Waleda had headed out with her basket and knife to collect some plants. She had spotted some mugwort a few days ago and thought it would be at its peak today. Eleanor slept in a little later these days, now that she was three full moons with child, and she knew Waleda was, more often than not, out picking plants, flowers, or herbs. Either that or she was in the barn working with what she had gathered. Therefore, it was no surprise when she awoke to a quiet house. Thomas had gone on one of his overnight travels. He was doing this more often now, as he told Eleanor that once their child was with them, he would be spending more time at home.

She padded downstairs and went to the fire to place the water on for some special tea that Waleda had her drinking upon rising. It quelled her morning queasiness and kept her feeling at peace. Hearing the door creak open, she said, "Oh good morning, Waleda. How was your morning foraging today? I was just about to make some food, would you like something?"

"That's awfully kind of you to offer. I think that would be lovely."

Startled by the stranger's voice, she nearly dropped the water and turned to see a tall, lean man with a scruffy beard and piercing blue eyes staring at her pregnant belly before bringing his eyes up to her face. Trying to sound brave, she asked, "Who are you and what is it you want?

The man only chuckled.

"My husband is out in the barn and will be coming into the house in a few minutes. Perhaps you would rather speak with him." Feeling vulnerable, she pulled her shawl tighter around her shoulders and protectively placed her hands on her stomach, which was just beginning to show.

Creavy noticed and chuckled again. Staring at her, he said, "Ah, now, I do know that what you 'ave just said is not true. Your 'usband, Thomas, is away until tomorrow evening, I believe. I think you 'ad best make me something to eat. You did offer that, did you not?"

Waleda was humming to herself as she approached the house. Ofttimes, she went straight to the barn, but since she had been gone a bit longer, she thought it wise to check on Eleanor first. As she stepped up onto the porch, she heard a deep voice within.

"Where is that 'ealer lady everyone talks about? I expected 'er to be 'ere. I was not expecting you, but... I am pleased that you are 'ere. The wife. Even better."

Eleanor busied herself, trying to put a meal together, "It is not her day to be here. She comes only a few days a week. If it is she you seek, I can go and get her for you. She lives very nearby." She tried to make her way to the door, in pretence of fetching Waleda.

Creavy jumped up from his bench, knocking it over, and grabbed her by the wrist. Eleanor screamed. He struck her hard on the cheek and told her if she tried that again he would make her very sorry. He also added that, unless she wished to have her child beaten out of her, she had best be silent and only answer his questions. She whimpered in agreement and sat on the chair, one hand holding her stinging face, the other upon her belly.

Waleda stopped herself from running into the room when she heard the scream and scuffle inside.

You must think, she told herself. It is the only way to save Eleanor. She listened for a moment and nearly gasped when she overheard what was said next.

Recovering just enough, Eleanor asked, "Who are you and what is it you want from us?"

"Ah, now, being that there is a price upon my 'ead, it might not seem wise for me to tell you my name. But since you will not be leaving 'ere to claim a reward… ever, I am Creavy. I am a businessman and I 'ave some business with your 'usband. I 'ave waited a long time for this business transaction to take place. Besides, I believe you and I can find many ways to pass the time until your 'usband returns. I 'ave so many tricks up my sleeve when it comes to the ladies." He licked his lips before continuing. "The 'ealer was 'ow I found you. Folks talk about these things you know. 'ealer. Stays with Thomas. You know 'ow it goes. I waited and listened. Now, you 'ad best be gettin' on wif making me some food. My temper does not improve if I am 'ungry."

No one else was expected here today, so Waleda knew it was down to her alone. She backed away with care and headed to the barn to devise and organize a plan.

Having gathered what she needed, she made her way across the yard, singing in a loud voice so that

Eleanor and the intruder would know she was coming. She pushed open the door, kept her head down whilst rummaging through her basket, and said, "Hello, dear Eleanor. I thought I would come by and bring you some more herbs for your pregnancy and then we can go and visit old farmer Thistle." Then acting surprised at seeing Creavy she said, "Oh my. I did not realize you had any company. Perhaps you would care to join us for some tea and then you can accompany us to the farmers cottage?" she asked him.

Creavy looked at Eleanor and then at this silver-haired lady who had just come in. "You must be the silver lady they speak of in the villages. The 'ealer. I thought you were not expected today. Mmmm?"

"Oh, I am almost never expected. I just pop in when it feels right, when the sun and moon have aligned for me. Now, would you like that tea? I am going to have some, and then we will depart." She set about heating the water and gathering a pestle and mortar to grind her tea. She caught Eleanor's eye and tried to give her an encouraging look, a look to tell her everything would be alright. She just needed to remain calm. No mention was made of Eleanor's swelling purple cheek, as she did not want to anger Creavy any more. However, she worried it might be suspicious, so she began to chatter about how poor her eyesight was. "What with all of these tinctures and potions I make up, you'd think I could mix up something for myself to help me see better. Ah well, never mind."

She continued grinding her herbs into a paste and then added some to two cups before pouring water in and whisking each cup into a frothy drink.

"Now, my dear Eleanor cannot be drinking this tea because it just might bring her baby to us sooner than we want it to, but you and I can certainly enjoy it. I picked this only this morning, and it is always best when it is fresh." Handing him his cup, she said, "Oh, I do apologize for not introducing myself. My name is Waleda, and who might you be?"

"Now why would I tell you my name, you old witch?"

She looked deep into his eyes, squinting to keep up the pretense of poor vision, and said, "Oh, no matter then. I already know your name. It is Creavy." She was pleased that she had slightly unsettled him. "Now, let us enjoy our tea before we discuss what it is that brings you into the home of my friends."

"You first," he said, nodding towards her drinking vessel. His piercing eyes followed her like a hawk as she took a sip. Then he began drinking his.

They drank in silence as Eleanor cried.

33

She must act as though nothing was unusual. Alaria knew this was of the utmost importance. Nine days had passed since her conversation with Banton about her suitor, so she knew the day was fast approaching. She and her father had been keeping track of all the guard changes, how long there was only one guard at their door, or none, which seemed to happen more frequently. It seemed most energy and effort was being put into the king's travel arrangements, so their security was relaxed. She could not afford to arouse any suspicion at all with any of their guards or captors, however, so she put on an act of contrition whenever a meal was brought in by one of the women.

Ever since she had told her father there was the possibility of an escape, he was becoming more self-assured. He was a shadow of the man he had once been yet seemed to grow a little stronger every day. Alaria knew he would never be able to walk with the confidence and royal stature he once held so naturally. Even so, she was sure he would be a balm for the villagers who had remained loyal to him. They had been able to piece together bits and pieces from overhearing the guards' conversations, so they knew many villagers had been starved due to an unfair distribution of food. Many had been run out of their homes, forced to flee their lands, for fear of reprisals and death. Any who wished to remain alive paid exorbitant taxes and pledged their allegiance to King Traintor. These overheard snippets also revealed that the super elite's wealth had increased since Oshinor had been overthrown. They may not embrace a king returning them to their old ways, releasing their slaves, and sharing a decent portion of their wealth throughout society where it was needed. Still, Oshinor felt deep down inside that some of them were good, decent people and prayed they had been pledging their fealty to Newark simply as a ruse. Others he knew had most likely assisted in him being overthrown and the kingdom being taken over by their now despicable leader. He feared them the most.

Late at night, after Soria was asleep, Alaria and her father met up to discuss their observances.

"Father, I believe that once Newark leaves the castle, which is tomorrow, those remaining will be either relieved he has gone so they can let their guard down, so to speak, or… they will be angry they've been left behind and therefore, possibly, willing to assist us."

"I've been thinking much the same. I've noticed one of the guards, Blinken, I believe he is called, doesn't even try to disguise his disgust and hatred for Newark. If he freely speaks of this with those around him, they must hold similar feelings, as we know if they did not, Blinken would have been removed and killed already. I will speak with him tomorrow."

"Do you think that wise, Father? What have we to offer him to not betray us?"

"My daughter, I can offer him a position of power for his loyalty to us, once we are back on the throne. Many men desire power of some sort, and with the promise of an earldom and some land, why would he betray us? I'll even write it out and sign it for him."

"Thank you for trying to save us and put our lives back together. I know we do not speak of it often, but I love you and Soria dearly."

King Oshinor let his tears flow freely as he took Alaria into his arms. "My dearest, I love you also, but you should know that you, not I, are the reason we will become free. Your will, strength, cunning, and perseverance are the reasons we are still alive and preparing to take back what is rightfully ours. As I promised, you will jointly lead this kingdom with me, right by my side. I am so very proud to call you daughter."

34

"You witch!" Creavy stumbled out of his chair. He tried to stand but staggered into the table, knocking all the dishes onto the floor. "What... 'ave...you... done?" Clutching his chest with one hand, he tried covering his eyes from the light. He was delirious now, completely incoherent.

Waleda had been sipping her tea whilst Creavy emptied his cup. It tasted deliciously sweet. That would be the berry she added for flavor. It was the fresh root that was deadly. Knowing she would soon be having a reaction also, she reached into her pocket for the Calabar beans and swallowed two of them whole, careful not to bite into them.

Eleanor was becoming hysterical and hurried over to Waleda who could not quite focus on her face.

"Sweet Eleanor. Do not fret. I have taken something to help me. Whatever you do, do not touch any of the leaves in my basket. They will cause your skin to blister. Do not touch that horrible man either. Just in case."

Between sobs, Eleanor said, "Waleda. No, no, no. You have poisoned yourself to save us. Please tell me what I can do to help you?"

Waleda staggered to the door and leaned off the porch to wretch. She vomited with such force, she brought up blood. "Don't get any of it on you," she rasped to Eleanor, who was trying to hold her upright. "The best thing now is to let me lie down. I need another Calabar bean, as I've most likely dispelled the others. Please fetch me water and let me crawl inside myself. I do not want to risk you getting poisoned."

After swallowing another bean and drinking some water, Waleda pulled herself along the floor before lying nearby to Creavy. He was convulsing and frothing at the mouth.

She looked at him and smiled as she said, "You are dying, Creavy. Your heart feels like it is jumping out of your body. You are thirsty. You are confused. I had always thought I would seek you out and make you pay for what you did to my daughter." She almost laughed when she said, "But you came to me. You came to me." Then she began to cry. "Yes, you will die. I... may also die. But even if I do, it will have been worth it. My sweet Mildrea did not deserve the life you made her live. No, she did not deserve that."

As the old woman's eyes began to glaze over, Eleanor cupped her head in her hands, careful to use her shawl and not touch her skin. "Waleda. Waleda. You listen to me. You will not die. I will not let you. I am here, my friend. I will care for you."

Turning to Creavy, Waleda kicked his boot to arouse him before shouting, "This is for Rose!"

Creavy blinked as he tried to focus on her face. "Rose? Is that you, Rose?" Then he passed out.

It was midday a few days later when Thomas arrived home. Something felt off, but he couldn't quite figure out why. There was quiet all around. And though the hens were clucking and scratching at the earth as usual, something seemed amiss. He couldn't put his finger on it, but his gut was stirring. He unhitched the horses from the cart and led them into the barn.

Where was Waleda? He usually heard her before he saw her, singing or humming as she mixed up her potions in the barn. Perhaps she was in the house supping with Eleanor. Then he noticed her fire was not lit. That was very strange. Walking around to the back of his house, he saw a strange horse tied up, causing the hairs on the back of his neck to stand on end. Knowing that Creavy was hunting him, he felt an overwhelming fear for his wife and the dear old silver-haired lady who had come into their lives.

He wanted to charge inside but worried that if Creavy were in there with the women, it could be deadly. Instead, he opened the door with great care and entered the house. The fire was crackling away, but where was everyone? He heard a creak on the stairs, of someone descending. Crouching into a shadowy corner, he froze, ready to pounce.

Eleanor screamed and nearly dropped the tray she was carrying when Thomas flew out of the corner.

"Oh my darling, I'm so sorry. I did not mean to frighten you. Is everything alright?"

She began to cry, and he led her over to sit down as he kissed her head and tried to calm her. She explained what had happened and how she had been tending to Waleda. She went in and out of delirium, but Eleanor hoped her fever had finally broken. She had to be very careful though, as before slipping into near unconsciousness, Waleda had been quite clear Eleanor could not get any of her sweat, saliva, or vomit on her or it could harm the baby.

"Oh, Thomas, I've carried our child this long, longer than any of the others. I cannot bear to lose them now!" At this, she completely broke down, and Thomas held her closely while she sobbed.

He learned that, although Eleanor didn't want to involve anyone else, she knew she could not get Waleda into bed without help, so she first dragged Creavy by his boots, put him out back, and threw a blanket over him. Just doing that took her the better part of the day. It was beginning to get dark when she went to their neighbor's cottage to ask for assistance. Farmer Thistle and his son came and carried Waleda upstairs to her bed. She told them to wash themselves, as she did not know what ailed Waleda, and she made sure they had done so before they left.

"Thomas, I have been so careful. I only hope I haven't accidentally done anything to harm our child. I also do not know if Waleda will ever recover. She poisoned herself! That wretched man died a horrendous death, and I feared the same would happen to her. I've tended to her the best I can, but she doesn't seem to be stirring much."

"There, there, love. I'm here now. You have been so strong and brave, but now let me care for you. I'll check on Waleda, and then I'll see to the scoundrel outside." He took her in his arms and held her tightly. It took all his willpower not to scream out his fear and hatred for the pain Creavy had caused. When he had composed himself enough to hide these feelings from Eleanor, he walked up the stairs to Waleda's bedroom.

He stood outside of the door for a moment and took a deep breath. He smiled when he heard, "Come in. You've woken me now, you may as well just enter."

Overcome with relief, he shouted, "Eleanor! She's awake! She's awake!"

He then entered to see Waleda lying on the bed. She was pale, her face matching her hair color. She looked just this side of death, and he understood Eleanor's fear. There was a chair near the fire, and he hoisted it in an arch with one hand and sat upon it right next to the bed, in a move that would've made a circus performer jealous.

"You must be either a cat or a witch, woman… You certainly seem to have many escapes with death."

Waleda smiled and asked if Eleanor and the babe were alright.

It had taken Eleanor a little time to walk up the stairs because her legs were shaky and her belly felt heavy, but she poked her head around the door to hear Waleda ask about her. "Yes, yes, we're fine. I have been so worried about you. I cannot believe what you did. It was a foolish thing to do. I am grateful to you for saving my life, though." She could barely get the last words out as she began to cry.

"My dear sweet Eleanor, come, sit on my bed. You no longer need to fear me being toxic to you and your child."

Eleanor laid her head on Waleda's lap and cried. She had much to cry for. Her baby kicked a few moments ago, which made her feel joy, and this woman who had cared for her, Thomas, and their child, who had read stories to her, and who, beyond a doubt, saved her life, was awake and talking as though everything would be perfectly fine.

As Waleda stroked Eleanor's head, she smiled at Thomas.

"Thank you," he said through his own tears.

"No thanks needed. You saved me once. It was the least I could do."

35

Once Bracknor explained to the gathered villagers why and how they should proceed sooner with their plan, a palpable intensity seemed to spread throughout the village. The atmosphere was one of solemnity but also excitement at the prospect of having decent lives again, no longer ruled by a tyrant. He also reminded everyone in the village that it was possible the royal family may no longer be alive. "Even if we are not able to rescue them, we will overtake the castle and overthrow the traitor king when he returns from his travels. In this way, we will regain our lives."

There was silence as he said this.

He searched the crowd for Dandy, and when their eyes locked, she smiled at him to let him know she understood just how dangerous this would be. "Now, we get to work."

Preparations were under way. Some people began packing up the needed food supplies whilst the others organized their weaponry. It was anticipated that they could gather up everyone in their rescue party within a few days, and once the first bonfire was lit, it would be a matter of only five or six days until they stormed the castle. Should all be successful, they would be returning home in about ten to twelve days. Bracknor knew even the best plans were often derailed, and they needed to prepare for at least a fortnight away.

It was all happening so fast that it almost felt surreal. Each village they arrived at, more people joined in their crusade. Yes, it was a rescue mission for King Oshinor and his family, who they hoped were still alive, but it felt more like a crusade. The night was bright. The moon was not quite full yet, but shadows were long on the ground. They would slowly ride into each village, their horses' breath and the breath of the farmers on foot misting in the cool night air. There was always the possibility of an ambush from Newark's men, so they needed to be alert. One or two men would enter a village first, and then upon hearing the special howl, they would answer, wait for a response, and then all enter. Bracknor couldn't believe how many farmers were joining them. These were not soldiers, just hardworking people who were tired of being abused by unscrupulous power. They and their families were facing starvation, and something needed to change. For this reason, they joined in the rescue crusade.

When they were about three hours away from the castle, Bracknor sent messages through the men that they would be resting up for the night. He knew of a place where he had often rested his troops before returning to the castle. King Oshinor always wanted his soldiers to return in daylight so the citizens could honor them if they had been victorious and support them and grieve with them if they had not. They could stay there for the night and most of the next day whilst he sent out scouts to make sure Newark and his soldiers had departed, leaving the castle vulnerable. The spot was far enough from the main road and near an ever-flowing creek, so they could partake of provisions and even light fires without being seen and arousing suspicion. This group of around four hundred brave souls, united in their purpose, made their way off the road to settle for the night.

A gentle din arose from the encampment. There were shared meals and the aroma of stewing vegetables along with soft relaxed laughter that permeated the crisp night air. There was the occasional spit with a rabbit or some other animal roasting. The animal had been startled and shot with an arrow on their journey, but most of these people had very little to eat apart from root vegetables and whatever herbs and wild lettuces they could gather along the way. The occasion felt festive, in that gatherings were no longer permitted and here were several villages mingling and catching up on one another's lives, however measly they had been under the current ruler. They were sharing whatever morsels they could. Some were braiding each other's hair, adding flowers and feathers. Others were sharpening arrowheads and tightening bow strings, or sharpening axe heads and other homemade weapons.

Bracknor was pleased. This felt good. This felt right. Seeing and hearing everyone happy again, acting human again, this was the reason for them to be doing what they were about to do. He only hoped they would succeed because he knew if they didn't, it could mean a torturous death for all of them. These simple folk who only wanted better lives. Mustn't think about that, he told himself as he headed over to speak with the village delegates.

This group wasn't like any of those he'd just walked through. This gathering was consumed with seriousness and concern. They knew what their plan was, but they wanted to go over it again and again, until everyone involved in leading their villagers felt as prepared as possible. They felt a grave responsibility, as if they may be leading them into death. It felt akin to going into battle. Bracknor explained what each of them were to do again. He knew how afraid they were. He was afraid also, and he'd been in many battles. These folks were farmers, craftsmen, and women, simple folk. Finally everyone settled.

Bracknor cleared his throat. "Now, I know that fear you are all feeling. I am feeling it too. Let me remind you that you have survived four horrible years under one of the worst tyrants we've ever known. This is why we're all here, why we are all risking our lives and those of our villagers who have remained at home. If we carry on as we've been doing, well…" He looked around at their serious gaunt faces. "Well… we most likely won't last through another cold season. We all know this, and that is why we must rescue King Oshinor and his family… should they still be alive." A lump formed in his throat. Mentioning his friend's name, he felt the anger and guilt of running away and leaving him. He knew that he had to do it or he would have been strung up, but he still deeply regretted sneaking out of the castle the way he had.

The villagers waited for him to compose himself. By now they had heard who this man was, which is why they had chosen to follow him.

Looking around at each of them, he said, "Now, go back to your encampments, enjoy being with your people tonight. They've come on this road with us, and they need to feel confident in your leadership. So for tonight, eat, laugh, enjoy their company. Tomorrow we will share our strategy and finalize any supplies and preparations before heading out at dusk. Let us meet up here tomorrow when the sun is on high."

There were kind, firm hands on shoulders and pats on the backs as they all dispersed, murmuring amongst themselves. Bracknor watched them go and thought they were some of the bravest people he had ever known.

36

Waleda had recovered enough to get up and go downstairs. The house was quiet, and she wondered where Eleanor was. Thomas had left a few days ago to join the villagers storming the castle to rescue King Oshinor and his royal family. He promised Eleanor he would not be involved in the fighting. He only wished to use his knowledge of the courtyard layout and entrances to assist the man leading the rescue, a man named Bracknor. Apparently he had been the most noble soldier to Oshinor but managed to escape when the kingdom was overthrown, and he'd been laying low the past four winters in Vintnos. Now he was all everyone in the villages could speak of. Thomas figured he had been gone for so long that he may need more recent information, and it didn't feel right to sit by and wait.

Going to the fire to put some water on for tea, Waleda heard a noise just outside the front door. She opened it and saw Farmer Thistle's two sons standing there.

"Good morning. I understand I need to thank you and your father for carrying me up to my bed when I had fallen ill. Come in, please. Would you like some tea? I am just brewing it up."

The older son would barely look at her, but his brother, whom Waleda did not know quite as well, said, "We won't be having any tea today. Neither will you. We need you to come with us. Do so quietly, and you will not be hurt."

She did not understand what was happening but remained calm when she said, "Alright. Let me just gather my shawl for traveling. Where is it that we are going? Do I need my herbs? Is someone ill or injured? At the least, I need to tell Eleanor where I have gone."

The brothers looked at each other. Her kindness was throwing them off. Finally, the older one spoke. "Miss Eleanor is at our home right now. Our mother came and collected her this morning. We will look after her until Thomas returns. You needn't worry about her."

"I do not understand. Please explain to me what is happening."

He was uncomfortable but continued, "'Tis nothing personal, milady, but after my father and I carried you upstairs, we heard a horse whinnying around the back of the house. We knew the master was away with his horses, so we went to see about the animal we heard. What we saw was a dead man, on the ground, covered with a blanket. We have both seen posters of this man. He had a price upon his head, dead or alive. After much discussion, we planned on bringing our wagon back a few days later and taking the body ourselves to get the gold. Unfortunately, Thomas had already come home and dealt with the man, burying or burning him, we do not know."

Now the younger boy spoke. "Without the body, we cannot claim the reward. So we will both swear we saw him here, which my father and brother did. We will say he was alive and that you murdered him, and we saw his body. That way we will be able to collect the money."

"So, you will be turning me over for the murder of a wanted man, even though you were originally going to say that you killed him yourselves?"

Neither man answered nor looked at her. Truth be told, the older brother feared Waleda. He had seen her using plant remedies on both humans and animals. He knew she was able to heal. He had also listened to some of the other villagers who were suspicious of her and called her a witch.

Sighing and resigned, Waleda said, "I understand. Please tell Eleanor and Thomas that I am sorry for involving them in this. Let me just gather a few of my things for our journey, please." With that, she walked up the stairs. She had not fully recovered and found the climbing slow going. She had always told herself she may die avenging her daughter's death. When she had managed to kill Creavy and survive, she hoped that was the end of it. Ah well, if it was to end this way, so be it. What saddened her the most would be missing the birth of Eleanor and Thomas's child. She was sure it was a girl but told neither of them, of course.

She came back downstairs and walked to the barn, explaining that she needed to collect a few things. They went into the barn with her and saw her herbs drying and several other unidentified plants and bits in boxes or clay containers. She sensed their nervousness and said, "I am only taking plants to aid us in case anyone feels ill with stomach pains, cramp, muscle soreness from traveling, an animal or insect bite. I just like to be prepared."

What they did not know was that she was also taking the same poison she had killed Creavy with,

Atropa belladonna, though this time she did not have the Calabar beans as an antidote. She made a pact with herself that if things got too difficult, she would ingest the berries and end it all. Hopefully it would not come to this, but she wanted to be prepared.

"Well then, let us be on our way. Am I to ride in the back of your wagon, or are we going on horseback? I do know how to ride."

The men agreed that riding on horseback would be quicker than taking the wagon, so they left it in front of the house and set off on their journey. Each rode their own mount, and they flanked the silver-haired lady, as if she was a prisoner. Waleda looked back over her shoulder for a memory of where her most recent home had been. It seemed like every time she settled down and felt happy, the world had other ideas and would send her into upheaval. She smiled at the irony of it all and hoped that at least the villagers would be successful in rescuing King Oshinor and helping their kingdom return to a place of kindness, fairness, and decency.

37

Arising from sleep felt like pushing through a thick fog for Bracknor. It had been a heavy night. Not heavy in sleep but heavy with the weight of today. The day of justification was upon them. Today they would storm the castle and search for the royal family. Of course, he wished for success, yet he was also filled with fear and dread. What if they were too late? What if his friend no longer survived or had been tortured? What if a trap was waiting for them on the other side of the walls? He had no way of knowing what to expect and he wouldn't put anything past Newark.

He dare not share his thoughts with these folks. Somehow, even during this difficult time, he had managed to bring together several villages. People had been terrified, unsure how to survive, and now they were rising up and marching against the very man and his army who had been keeping them living a meager existence, knowing the slightest move or wrong word would get them killed. They had enough and were at breaking point, so here they were. Expecting Bracknor to lead them to a victory of sorts against this evil king and restoring peace and fairness to the Kingdom of Welexia was all they could believe in at the moment. They had worked hard these past four days together, learning combat maneuvers, learning to trust complete strangers. That in itself was a victory, as they hadn't even trusted their own neighbors out of fear of Newark and his spies. Considering these were frightened farmers, many of whom had never even ventured out of their own village, made it all the more spectacular. They were all here with a shared purpose of getting their lives back. No fires would be lit today. It meant a day of eating cold hard bread, fruit, and jerky. A current of excitement and eagerness was in the air. Bracknor knew these men and women hadn't held their heads up this high in years. They had been living without expectation and now they were filled with it. It was wonderful.

 He also felt as though he had been unshackled from his own imprisonment of living as Whistler, a farmer. Keeping his secret had brought him his love, Dandy, and it had saved his life, but it always felt wrong to sit by and not fight. Many nights he lay awake wondering about his friend and king, Oshinor. He had believed the royal family must have been slain but had always held onto a glimmer of hope they might still be alive. When he learned they were, he could not sit and wait any longer. He would have ridden into the castle walls himself if it meant he could try to rescue his friend. He was a soldier through and through, and the wait had been almost unbearable. At last, the time had come, and he was ready for it, no matter what the outcome.

An approaching horse snorted, jolting him from his thoughts. He looked up to see a man who looked healthier and stronger than most of the other villagers. He actually looked like someone the king would want in his army because of his physical stature.

The man spoke. "Whistler?"

Bracknor's thoughts whirled. *Can I trust this man? I don't want all of this preparation to be lost on a spy. Especially now that we are so close to the castle.* Trying to look as relaxed as possible, he said, "How can I help you, friend?"

"My name is Thomas, and I've come to help. I visit the castle grounds frequently, selling my wares. I think I'd be a good asset to getting inside. I know the perimeter quite well. I don't want to join the fight because my wife is home with child, and I promised her that I wouldn't..."

Their eyes took in one another. Thomas was sure this was the man he needed to speak with. He also understood his mistrust.

"Wait here with these men. I'll speak with Whistler and then return to you."

Thomas nodded in agreement.

Bracknor approached some of his men. "Keep an eye on that villager. Try to be subtle, but make sure he does not leave."

If he was a spy, Bracknor needed him to stay here. He didn't mention anything to his men about Thomas being a potential spy. He didn't need them to start breaking ranks now and fleeing out of fear.

For his part, Thomas knew he was being watched. He tried making small talk, but the men were awkward and he was making them nervous. He decided the best thing to do would be to simply wait. But he must be ready to jump on his horse and ride away should things take a turn.

Bracknor gathered up a few delegates and asked if any of their scouts had returned from the castle. So far none had. Then he asked if any of them knew of a vendor named Thomas.

Gyles stepped forward. "Yes, he visited my village. He was searching for friends of mine to deliver a note from their daughter, who had been held captive in a brothel in the castle."

"Gyles, isn't it? Would you recognize him again?" asked Bracknor.

"Yes, I believe I would. He is a large man, rather tall."

"Alright, you come with me. The rest of you stay here and wait for your scouts to return. Please come find me as soon as they do."

Once Gyles told Bracknor he recognized Thomas, the men discussed all entrances into the castle, including the main and vendor entrances. Thomas was also able to tell Bracknor about things that had changed on the interior and the perimeter in the four summers since he'd been there. It was agreed that Thomas would accompany them to the castle, but he wanted little to do with the fighting, should any take place, as he would soon be a father.

Bracknor smiled and said, "You say your wife is with child? Mine is also. I will respect your wishes, but I ask that you stay by my side as much as you are able until we get inside."

"I can agree to that. And congratulations to you, sir." Thomas nodded.

The men then set about preparing for what was to come later in the day.

It was around midday when a scout returned with news that Newark and his entourage had left the castle for their village tour three days ago, heading north. From there, they would head westward then turn back inland and head south. They anticipated being gone a fortnight or perhaps a few days longer. There was no need to remain in each village any longer than it took for adoration and tax collection. The tour had been broadcast as a blessed visit from their leader, a time to put on one's finery, lay the tables with the finest food and wine, bring on the music, dancers, jugglers, and any and all entertainers.

The reality was that only the wealthiest landowners would be able to put on such a show. Even then, they would be doing it behind locked gates within their walled estates. The farmers and peasants had been told to line the roads and cheer for the king as he went past. Failure to do so would mean a public whipping followed by a hanging or crucifixion, whichever the king desired. Even if they fooled the king, if the landowners didn't feel they had abided by their terms, they would be following up after he had left with punishment of their own. Most of the wealthy were out of touch with just how severely starving their tenants were and had no idea of the living conditions surrounding their safe abundant homes. A few, however, did know how precarious things were, and because of this, they knew the balance of power could shift at any time if the peasants decided to turn on them. They could see the hunger, fear, and hatred in their eyes and knew that when people felt this way, they were dangerous.

As scouts continued to return with any news they had gleaned, Bracknor and his delegates discussed necessary changes to strategy. When news got back to them that Newark wouldn't be stopping for longer than one night in each village, it was a little unsettling, only because this meant the soldiers would never fully unpack. Therefore, they could easily make haste back to the castle if news of a rebellion reached them. There was much discussion amongst them. It was becoming a little prickly when Bracknor interrupted them all.

"Not to worry friends. We know this king changes his mind and his plans easily. Yes, it means he is unpredictable, but we can use this to our advantage. It also means he is disorganized. Even if his army attempts to keep everything orderly, their king, by his nature, keeps them disheveled. A disorganized army is not to be feared. They fall apart and crumble easily. I have also heard that many are only loyal to save their lives and the lives of their families."

Upon hearing these words, a murmuring went up amongst the assembled villagers.

"Now, before we judge them too harshly, we must ask ourselves if we wouldn't have done the same, if placed in their situation."

"Never! I would be loyal, even at the cost of death to my family and myself!"

A silence rested upon them as they looked around to see who had spoken these words. It was Hortence, from one of the villages in the farthest reaches of the kingdom. Some of the men snorted with disbelief at what he had said.

Bracknor knew he must diffuse the situation, so he looked him firmly in the eyes when he said, "It is serendipitous that we have you fighting with us and not against us, Hortence. Thank you for your passion and commitment." He continued, "Men, women, let us take it upon ourselves and all who follow us to enter our castle, free our true king, release any others unrightfully locked up, and do so with compassion. If anyone remaining to guard the castle lowers their weapons and agrees to side with us, let us allow them to do so. We need people to be united, not divided as we have been for the past four years, even longer if we look at how the seeds of hatred and division were planted by Newark and his followers. We need to be side by side and not stabbing one another in the back. We can do this. We will do this. I believe we will succeed. Let us return to our groups and get into formation, for dusk approaches in due course and we must be in place to enter the castle as we have planned. May the power of the harvest gods, the moon goddesses, and all other gods you believe in be with us all."

38

Oshinor, Alaria, and Soria had just finished eating, and Alaria knocked on the door to see if anyone was there. When she received no reply, she resumed her seat with her family. She had suggested to her father that they let Soria know they were planning an escape. They wanted her to feel prepared. As prepared as possible anyway.

Oshinor began speaking. "Soria, you know that your sister and I have private conversations oftentimes. It is not that we wish to hide things from you but we have done so more for your protection."

Rolling her eyes, Soria said, "Yes, I am very aware that you two whisper over there near the small window. You think I am busy studying or drawing and that I take no notice, but I do." She seemed almost hurt.

The king looked to Alaria to continue.

"Sister, we have something to tell you now. It involves all three of us, and it may be dangerous. Most likely it will be. Shall I say more?"

Soria, now looking like a very young frightened child, nodded her head for Alaria to continue.

Alaria inhaled deeply and said, "Well, a few nights from now, my virtue is to be sold to a man I do not know. And then, once I am tarnished, I will continue to be sold out regularly."

She paused to let it sink in. She could see Soria was having a difficult time absorbing these words, yet she knew if she didn't tell her all then she may never be able to speak of it to her again, so she continued.

"Everything has been orchestrated by Banton. It is the reason we are living in better conditions. I made a deal with him."

Soria was silent, with tears running down her cheeks.

She went on. "I was concerned that you, father, and I would end up like our mother and Genison. I only wanted us to live." Alaria was crying now also, as was their father. She cleared her throat and dried her eyes. Composed once more, she said, "Obviously I do not wish this to happen, which is why father and I have been trying to figure out a way for us to escape from our imprisonment. We know that Newark and a great number of guards, soldiers, and his entourage have left the castle for a fortnight, and by listening very closely to chatter, we know that only a small number have been left here to guard us and protect the castle. This is our best time to attempt an escape."

Soria broke her silence and said, "Where will we go? How will we live?"

Oshinor spoke up. "We are not entirely sure where we will go once we escape, but we believe that if we can get to a village and reveal who we are, we may be able to convince some of the villagers to side with us and rise up against the usurper Newark. I know it seems a nearly impossible feat, but we are strong, my daughters. We have endured much hardship already, and we are still living. I know your mother would not wish for Alaria to meet this fate. A fate that would most likely be thrust upon you also before too long. We must at least try to do this. I am the king of Welexia. You are princesses. This is who we are. We are not some lowly prisoners, even though this is how we have been treated for far too long. I admit I was nearly completely defeated, but Alaria helped me to find my way out of the darkness. She is the reason we are eating well, we are clean, and you have your studies. We owe her our lives, and we owe it to her to at least try this. Would you not agree?"

Before anyone could say more, there was a commotion outside their door. Alaria motioned for them to be quiet and, taking her sister by the arm, led her over to the wall just next to the door. Their father followed, and they were now on either side of the doorway. King to the left, princesses to the right, all listening. The walls were thick, and it was difficult to make out specific words, but it seemed that a scuffle of sorts was taking place. After what seemed like ages, a silence befell the corridor. Alaria placed her ear to the door as the lock was being rattled and jumped back just as the door flung open, revealing Blinken. Banton lay on the floor.

"Is he dead?" asked the king.

"Nah, I just knocked him out. There's some sort of commotion at the main gate, and most everyone has gone there. I figured this was as good a time as any to get you out of here. You remember your promise to me though, don't you?"

"Of course, Blinken. I am forever grateful and will bestow you with all that I promised once we are safely away from here."

"Alright, get what you need, and let us depart. Quickly!"

Whilst her father and Blinken spoke, Alaria was already gathering the bundles she had put together over the last two days. She tied two of them around her waist and tossed the third to their father. She had wanted to be prepared, to be ready, and now she was glad she was. Soria still seemed in a state of shock as Alaria took hold of her arm. The three of them followed Blinken down the dimly lit passageway. All the times that Alaria had made this journey to empty their privy pot, there had been many people about. Now it was eerie and quiet.

A mouse skittered across the floor, startling Soria, and she let out a small yelp. Well, that's good, thought Alaria, at least she is aware of her surroundings. She was concerned about her sister, as nothing they told her had time to sink in yet. There would be much to discuss later, but for now, they must escape and survive. Survival was all she could think of. She looked back to see her father right behind them. He was hawklike as he looked sharply around, surveying their surroundings and any potential threat.

For his part, Oshinor was tingling with fear and excitement. Something had indeed died within him during his captivity and the loss of his youngest daughter and queen, but feeling the possibility of freedom right now made him feel alive. Yes, he was the king, dammit! He needed to rule his people and guide them back to decent lives. He had overheard gossip and was able to glean how they were faring under Newark, but he had no idea of just how miserable their lives had been these past four years.

Blinken stopped short and waved them into silence. Not needed, as they had been silent the entire time they followed him. They all heard what he heard, however, and didn't protest when he opened a door and motioned them to go inside. He put up his hand, as if to say he would return, before closing the door and locking it from the outside.

It was pitch-black, and they were afraid to speak when they heard shuffling and chains scraping along the floor near them. Soria screamed as someone grabbed her by the ankle. It was happening so fast, no one really knew how to react. Alaria was having a tug of war, using her poor sister as the prize. Oshinor was fighting off someone else himself.

Alaria's mind was racing. *They can see us, so why can't we see them?* She closed her eyes to allow them to adjust, and when she opened them, she could see forms. They were in a room with several people. Everyone seemed to be chained to the walls. Only the two nearest could reach them.

Remaining calm, she said, "Father, try to get into the center of the room. They are chained to the walls and cannot reach us from there."

They continued struggling.

Alaria leaned into her sister and whispered, "Soria, kick him, kick him hard. Do it!"

Soria let out a guttural scream as she released a firm kick squarely into the head of this demonic person grabbing her leg.

They cried out and recoiled from the blow. Soria and Alaria nearly fell over when they let go, but Alaria quickly yanked her sister into the center of the room.

"Father, they are weak. Use your strength to kick them."

Oshinor kicked hard, and his leg was grabbed by his assailant. He fell upon his back, letting out a whoosh of air. Alaria told Soria to stay put as she hurried to his side. A rage overtook her, all four years of captivity and anger seeming to explode from her as she felt along the filthy floor for the chain of the one attacking her father. She grabbed it and yanked it with all her might. Everything was suddenly in slow motion. The person attached to the chain felt light as Alaria used their chain to swing them toward the wall. There was a sickening thud as they hit the wall and crumpled down into a silent stillness. She then reached out and helped her father crawl into the center, where the three of them remained huddled together.

39

"Who goes there?" asked the gate guard as Thomas approached a side entrance to the castle. This gate was usually only guarded by a single guard, sometimes two, but definitely not as many as were stationed at the main gate.

"Oh hello, friend, 'tis only me, Thomas the Tinkerman, trying to get a jump start on the morning crowd."

Bracknor and Gyles were squatting down on the far side of the wagon, away from the guard's sight. Whilst Thomas kept him talking, they squeezed inside the gate and made their way up the stone steps toward the guard. It was just getting dark, and the long shadows were making their ascension rather tricky. Slow and steady, Bracknor repeated in his head over and over.

The guard snorted. "Hmmph, not much of a crowd these days, what with so many traveling with the king."

"Yes, you must be sorry you weren't able to go out with them, instead of being stuck here."

"Nah, not really. It will be a nice break from all of the fawning and sycophantic behavior towards you know who," he chortled.

"Not a fan, then?" asked Thomas.

The guard's suspicions arose. Had he been careless with his tongue? Was this man a spy for King Traintor? His wife always told him it would be his big mouth speaking before thinking that got him into trouble. The guard unsheathed his sword. "Who did you say you were again?"

"No need to worry, friend. I am not a fan either. In fact, your honest thoughts have just saved your life," said Thomas as Bracknor and Gyles stepped out of the shadows.

Bracknor held his knife, and Gyles had a club in his hand. The guard released his sword and let it slide back into its sheath without hesitation.

"That's it. Nice and slow. Put your hands up where we can see them," said Bracknor.

He did as instructed, all the while his mind was racing with questions. Who were these men? What did they want? And why the feck did he have such a big mouth?

Bracknor stepped up, now face to face with the guard. "Now, what do you call yourself?"

"Hu-Hu-Hubert, sir," he stammered. It was what he did when he was nervous.

"Okay, good. Hubert, we are here for one reason only, and that reason is to rescue the king."

"Bu-bu-but I thought you just said… But wait, he is traveling… He don't need rescuing."

Bracknor waited for Hubert to compose himself before speaking. "The true king, King Oshinor."

Hubert's face contorted into something akin to surprise and preparation for vomiting.

"I see by your face that the rumors are true then." The sense of relief Bracknor felt was palpable as he exchanged nods and looks with Gyles and Thomas. "Ah, Hubert, this is your lucky night. You are going to help us with this rescue, and then you will be nicely rewarded. Now I bet you're glad we came along," said Bracknor as he slapped him on the back.

A distraction was about to take place at the main entrance to the castle. It needed to be unruly enough to bring out some extra guards as backup, but not so bad to cause any sword use from them. The rebellion, hidden amongst the early evening shadows, awaited the signal to get started. As soon as they heard a short cry akin to a male peacock followed by a torch swinging side to side three times, they were to begin.

Bracknor had instructed them to make a lot of noise with a lot of yelling over each other. There was to be some pushing and shoving for the front positions as they came out from the shadows, but it was mainly to cause confusion. The guards should not really know what they were yelling about, yet they should be wary of the rapidly swelling boisterous crowd. There were plenty of villagers able to fulfill this role. They needed to keep whatever weapons they had hidden closely next to them. They must appear to be unarmed, upset villagers, not an armed crowd ready to storm the castle. If you listened with care, you would hear a unified inhalation and exhalation of oxygen as their breathing fell into sync, but other than that, they were as quiet as a fox hiding in the bushes ready to pounce upon its unsuspecting prey.

The signal was given, and the crowd oozed out of the shadows. Their size and din grew as they did so. The guards were perplexed and couldn't figure out where all these people were coming from. They didn't draw weapons upon them, however, as these were weak villagers, surely no threat to them. They just needed to find out what it was they wanted so they could disperse them. All of their commanders had gone with the king, so even though there was meant to be a hierarchy, there wasn't any one person in charge. No one wanted to be responsible for making decisions. Someone had the bright idea to go and get the few soldiers left in the main building. They could come and tell them what to do. That way, if anything went wrong, the soldiers would be blamed, not the guards.

40

Oof, my fecking head is throbbing, thought Banton as he sat up rubbing it. He noticed the door to the king and princesses' room was wide open.

"No, no, no, no, no!" was all he could say as he felt his riches slipping away from him. "Where the feck are they, and who the feck laid me out like that?" A quick search of the room revealed no secrets, so he set off down the hallway with many questions and on the hunt for his most valuable prize, Alaria.

Blinken came upon soldiers he had heard a moment ago, just before locking the royals into a dark chamber. He tried to act casual as he asked what all the commotion outside was and whether it was sorted out. No one knew, but they could all hear the noisy crowd. They hurried outside onto a balcony to see several villagers who were now inside the gates.

Only a few torches had been lit, so it was difficult to make out what they were doing, but it was clear that a large group of people were pouring into the grounds. There seemed to be a never-ending stream of them.

Someone said, "Shite!" before dropping his sword and running off. Another ran off in the opposite direction. Before long, Blinken was on his own.

"Feck, feck, feck! What have I done? No one will believe me if I tell them I knew Oshinor was planning an escape and I wanted to hide him until King Traintor returned," he said to the thin air. He decided his best plan was to leave the castle and return to the village where he grew up. He would need to devise a good story though because, from what he remembered, those in his village were not fans of King Traintor. He'd think of that story later. For now, he needed to run.

He and Banton ran straight into each other.

"What happened?" asked Banton. "Someone hit me over the back of the head and then helped our royal captives escape. We must find them. Where did they go? Did you see them?"

Blinken was relieved when he realized Banton did not know it was him who whacked him over the head. "I don't know," Blinken lied. "They hit me too. When I saw you were knocked unconscious, I thought it best to try and find our captives, so I went off in search of them."

They both looked at each other and froze as they realized they heard many people coming down the hallway headed straight for them.

"We need to get out of here," shouted Banton. They ran off deeper into the castle, away from the rapidly approaching crowd.

The villagers had been instructed to branch out, entering every building and opening every door they could once inside the castle grounds. They should explain that they were there to rescue Oshinor and his family, to offer peace if possible, and only fight if anyone remained loyal to Newark. If a fight did occur, the objective was to capture those they fought. Death was to be a last resort. They had also been advised to release anyone they found living in the brothels. Tell them they were free to leave and return to their villages or join them and find new villages to live in.

Finding many of the castle doors unlocked meant the search was going rather well. They were met with very little resistance. Mostly people seemed relieved when they were told of the objective. A few broke down in tears of relief. Others were skeptical but felt pretty certain they shouldn't hang out and wait, so they grabbed whatever sparse belongings they could and injected themselves into the swelling crowd of villagers moving throughout the castle and grounds. A few people seemed to have lost their faculties and couldn't grasp what was happening. Some villagers took pity on them and led them out if at all possible.

The royal three were comforting one another when they heard a large crowd of people outside their chamber door. We either remain silent or alert someone to our presence, thought Alaria. The worst fate would be to be thrown into another locked up chamber and live out her days as Banton's sex slave. Before she had time to shout out, their door was being struck hard with a large object. There were cries in unison with each hit as it was being knocked in. They held their breath together. The door flew open, much to the surprise of those who had knocked it in. Cries of success went up but were soon followed by a silence that began at the doorway and melted throughout the crowd of people. One of the villagers stepped forward carrying a torch, which lit up the dark chamber.

"Milord, is it true? Can you be our King Oshinor?" asked Gyles.

King Oshinor pulled himself up tall as a redwood and replied, "Yes, it is true. Might I ask your name and your intention?"

Whispers were passed back to say they'd found the king. Disbelief amidst the joy. Was this really happening? The rumors had been true. Like a wave upon the sea, they all bowed low. Those able to went down on one knee. Alaria and Soria looked at one another as tears flowed down their cheeks.

Gyles, from his kneeling position, looked up, swallowed the lump in his throat, and said, "My lord, I am Gyles, sir. Our intention is to give you and your family your freedom again so that you can rule our kingdom... your kingdom."

Oshinor stepped forward and placed his hands upon Gyles's shoulders, lifting him to stand as he looked him in the eye. "But how did you know? How did you manage this?"

The crowd was parting as Bracknor walked through it to face his dearest friend. He felt a little unsteady on his feet as he tried to absorb the truth that Oshinor was standing in front of him. Both men stood as still as statues, never breaking eye contact, before Oshinor reached out to embrace his old protector and friend.

"It had to be you. I believed deep down that if anyone would help us, it would be you. I am so relieved you are alive."

Bracknor knelt down and said, "My king, your kingdom awaits you. Please, let me escort you outside so that everyone can see you and know that you and your family live."

Alaria stepped forward then and placed her hand on Bracknor's shoulder. "Please rise, valiant Bracknor. You may not remember me so well, but it is I, Alaria, and it is us who should be bowing to you."

Bracknor did as she said. "Of course I remember you." Looking back at her sister, he asked, "And your mother the queen, and your other sister?"

Alaria's downward-cast eyes told him all he needed to know.

He nodded to her and then turned to face the hushed crowd gathered in the corridor. "Friends of Welexia, loyal supporters of King Oshinor, let us continue on our mission to release captives within the castle wall. We will meet up in the center of the castle grounds. I will bring the king and his family out onto the balcony so that he can address everyone. Light as many torches as you can find to light up the night. Be on your guard, lest you encounter anyone who still holds loyalty to

Newark, but also know that we've done it. We've found our king!"

As he spoke the last words, the crowd erupted with whoops and yelps. People cried out in joyous cheers. Some even sang as they continued down the castle corridors in celebration to release and invite followers.

Those chained to the walls of the room slumped down, some crying. They were crying and apologizing to King Oshinor for attacking him and his family, explaining that they were starving and locked up as enemies of Newark. They asked for some torchlight and to have their chains broken.

As if four winters was merely a blink, Oshinor began dispensing orders to the few villagers who had remained with Bracknor. "Find a way to release these prisoners. Search for some food and water to give them."

The villagers couldn't believe the king was speaking directly to them. They were awestruck but responded to his commands. Bracknor asked Gyles to oversee their release and led Oshinor, Alaria, and Soria out of this chamber.

Alaria explained that they had a room not too far away and asked to go there so they could make themselves more presentable before addressing the crowd. Bracknor was pleased, though not surprised, at how grown up and confident she had become as he waved his hand for her to lead the way.

As they rounded the corner, they were met with three soldiers who held their swords at the ready.

Stepping in front of the royal family, Bracknor said, "Friends, we do not wish a battle. This is a day to celebrate and right the wrongs done to our king and the princesses. I ask that you lower your weapons and let us proceed. There will be a place for you in our king's army if you renounce Newark."

Without speaking, one of the soldiers lunged forward with his sword aimed at Bracknor's midsection. Bracknor anticipated the move and bent down low, swinging his arm back and then bringing his own sword forward and up, connecting with the soldier's weapon, sending it flying out of his hand. He then pivoted his body and pressed his sword under the chin of his opponent, stopping just before puncturing his throat.

"Shall we continue, or do you surrender this night?

The soldier said nothing but stepped back and spat on the ground. The other two motioned for him to come back to them.

"I ask you all one more time to join us. If you do not, and I see you again, you will be locked up until our king decides your fate. Now, place your swords on the ground and walk away."

After sharing looks with each other, the soldiers placed their swords on the ground.

Bracknor walked forward and retrieved them, handing them off to Alaria and the king. Then he approached each soldier to look at their faces so he could remember them in the future. "Be on your way now. I hope you find something useful to do as we prepare to return our king to his rightful throne."

They turned and walked away. Bracknor had expected some resistance and knew that, if determined, these three would've fought him with more conviction than this, so he wasn't worried.

41

News spread like wildfire that King Oshinor and his family had been rescued. They were indeed alive. The mission had been a success. Once all rooms in the castle had been searched and cleared out, everyone was to gather in the main courtyard so King Oshinor could address them. People were dancing and singing as they set about in preparation for a much-needed and long-awaited address from their true king, not the imposter who had made their lives miserable.

Thomas had been in the courtyard of the castle, watching and listening lest any of Newark's spies remained. From what he could tell, nearly all the soldiers were more than happy to lay down their arms and join in the rescue, which now felt festive. Just in case, they had villagers stationed as guards at each entrance and a few scattered within the grounds to catch any interlopers who might try to cause trouble. It was good to be with people because you chose to, not because you knew if you didn't, your family or you yourself would likely be killed.

Thomas did notice a few men set out on horseback away from the castle. It was inevitable that Newark would soon be alerted to what was happening. Bracknor had gone over the possible ways he felt Newark would react. Some of the stronger men must stay behind to protect those they had just freed, those who were not up for travel to their villages yet, and also those who had always lived within the castle grounds and would want to do so still. Tomorrow, plans would be made to pack up grains and supplies and head back to disperse them amongst their neighbors. Once a more permanent distribution was in place, everyone would have plenty to eat.

Bracknor's plan had succeeded, so Thomas went to the brothel to make sure no one had been left behind. He also felt he needed to have a look around so he could talk with Waleda about it. He knew she would want to know about the place her daughter had been living. He hoped to find something, any small thing of comfort, to take back and give to her.

There were a few women still mulling about, packing up some clothing, and wandering around dazed. They were having a hard time realizing they really could leave now and return to their villages or head out to new places and start again. It was a bit overwhelming. One of the women froze when she saw Thomas watching her.

"I'm sorry, miss, I did not mean to startle you. I had a friend who used to live here. She worked here, and well, she died, but I hoped to be able to tell her mother something about those she lived with. Perhaps you knew her. Her name was Mildrea, I mean Rose. Her name was Rose." He was composing himself when the woman came closer, and Thomas could see she was not much more than a child herself. He prayed she would not have known Mildrea, being so young.

Shyly she said, "No sir, I only just arrived two full moons ago. I didn't know your friend." Then her eyes welled up with tears, and she looked down at her feet as she continued, "I have nowhere to go. My father sold me when my mother and all of my siblings died of starvation. He wasn't well himself, and I don't think he'll be alive now. He thought I'd have a better life working in the castle. That's what he was told."

She sobbed now, and Thomas saw how frightened she was, so he reached out his hand towards her and told her it would be fine now. There would be food aplenty and she would no longer have to live this way. She continued looking at her feet but reached out and took hold of his strong safe hand.

"My name is Thomas. You can share your name with me, if you like, but it will be alright if you choose not to."

Glancing at him, still holding his hand, she said, "Before I came here, my name was Willow. I think I'd like to be Willow again."

He smiled and said, "Well then, Willow, shall we go outside and join the others?"

She nodded and they walked out together.

Inside the de facto royal room, Alaria and Soria assisted their father into looking as kingly as he could, given the clothing they had. They did their best to make themselves look presentable also. This would be the first time they stood before their people in over four long winters, and they wanted to look as regal as they could. Not for vanity but as a way to offer hope. Bracknor told them how much everyone had suffered and assured them they could come outside in torn rags and they would still be a balm for all.

Gyles entered to tell them the castle had been cleared. Everyone was set free. A few dissenters were being held in one of the prisons, but they were only a few. Some of the king's subjects were deathly ill and had been taken to a quiet wing of the castle, where they were being looked after. There was an assembly line sorting wagons and provisions and grains to be equally distributed once the king had finished addressing everyone. He also told them some farmers had arrived with a woman who they said had killed a wanted man. They wished to speak with someone about collecting the reward money.

Alaria felt something inside her gut and stepped forward, saying, "Please bring the men and the woman to me. I would like to speak with them."

Gyles nodded and sent a soldier to do as Alaria requested. A few minutes later, Waleda came into the room with Farmer Thistle's sons. They were all a bit overwhelmed, not quite able to believe they were being brought before royalty. As soon as Waleda saw King Oshinor and his daughters, she went down on her knees and bowed to them. She held her hands up to her face and cried tears of joy at seeing them alive. Alaria approached and asked her to rise.

She struggled a bit, as riding on a horse for a few days had made her joints a little stiff. "Pardon me. I am not as young as I once was, and I move less like a rabbit and more like a tortoise these days."

Alaria smiled at the silver-haired lady. "What is your name?"

"I am Waleda, milady. These gents have brought me here to claim reward money for a foul man who I killed. He tortured and then killed my daughter after treating her horribly for years. I have no regrets. If I am to hang for killing him, so be it."

Alaria then spoke to the young farmers. "Who is this man she has killed? You say there was a price upon his head and you wish to claim the reward?"

The older Thistle answered, "Yes. That is correct. We planned on bringing the man in alive," he lied, "but this woman killed him and then disposed of him. We saw him with our own eyes, but we do not know what she did with his body. Many around our village claim she is a witch, and that might explain the disappearance of a dead man. Which we both saw."

His brother quickly nodded in agreement with the lie.

"Well, since you did not answer my question of who he was, I shall ask Waleda the same question."

Waleda looked straight into Alaria's eyes and without shame said, "His name was Creavy, and he was a wicked evil man."

Alaria took a deep breath, remembering how he had frightened her when her family was first put into captivity. She had lived in fear over the years that Newark might send her and her sisters to be tamed by him. She stepped forward and placed her hands on Waleda's shoulders.

The women looked into each other's eyes, and Waleda understood that Alaria knew who this horrid man had been.

Not wishing to break down on what was turning out to be a most emotional day, she turned to the farmers saying, "Thank you for bringing this woman to us. When we have located our confiscated gold, you will be paid. Only a pittance, however, as it seems this woman did all of the hard work in killing Creavy, and you only wished to cash in on her labor. Once you have been paid, I would advise you to remain far away from the castle, as I do not care for people who try to make money off others unfairly." Then she turned to Gyles and said, "Please look after this woman. Creavy was indeed an awful human, and she has done us all a service in ending his life."

Waleda bowed in thanks. When she looked up, she saw Gyles was smiling at her with tears in his eyes. He held out his arm and then led her away to a private chamber. Both grateful that her life had been spared.

Oshinor had been observing his daughter as she assumed the role of a ruler effortlessly. She was fair and just, as he knew she would be.

Bracknor then turned to the king. "Well, your majesty, this is it. It is time. You have been sorely missed."

The king nodded and motioned for his daughters to flank him on either side. "My princesses, we survived. Your mother would be so proud of you both. Let us step up to this task and get our kingdom back to what it was. No, let us make it even better than before."

The cries were deafening as King Oshinor, Princess Alaria, and Princess Soria stepped out onto the balcony. King Oshinor thought it might not be very regal of him, but he openly wept tears of joy, as did his daughters and many of his subjects. Alaria caught Bracknor's eye and bowed her head in thanks. She knew they had a monumental task ahead of them, but felt more than ready. As she looked out over the crowd of roaring people, she was excited to begin.

EXCERPT OF BOOK TWO IN THE WELEXIA SERIES

The horse's nostrils flared shooting steam into the frosty morning air. The horse was exhausted, yet he was in better shape than the horseman, as he was a fresh mount from a village half a day away. The frantic horseman had been riding for at least two full nights, not counting the night he departed.

On that night, the guard realized something was happening, but unsure as to what it was, inserted himself into the crowd gathered in the castle courtyard, hoping to learn what was going on. He could not believe his eyes when a thin, gaunt King Oshinor with two Princesses flanking him addressed a packed castle courtyard. People were crying and hugging one another. People had been terrified of everyone for the past four and a half years and now they were celebrating together. How was this possible? Had not

King Oshinor fled the castle as King Traintor had told the people? How was he standing before them now?

After disbelief, then realization of the truth, bile rose from his stomach and he wretched., trying to keep his stomach contents from spewing everywhere. Thinking of all the villagers he had killed, or been witness to their murder, for even speaking the name Oshinor, his heart pounded. Would these villagers turn on him and tell their rescued king of the atrocities he had committed? Someone must alert King Traintor to what was happening in his absence. At least if I side with him I'll be looked after for my loyalty, he thought. Leaving the cheering crowd, he made his way to the stables and found a good solid mount to take him off into the night. Slowing down only to leave exhausted horses and get onto a fresh one, he arrived just after dawn, having lost track of how many days he had been riding.

The encampment was just beginning to awaken when he came galloping into it. Slow down and walk, he told himself. I don't want to alarm anyone. Trying to look as nonchalant as possible he trotted through the camp. His adrenaline was the only thing keeping him atop his horse as both his body and brain were exhausted. Riding hard had not kept the horrific scenes of torture from his mind. Had he done those things to innocent people in the name of King Traintor? He felt shame creeping in and knew it must be buried. He was but a guard following orders. Everything he had done was for his king. He told himself it was all right, that everything would be fine.

People were gathering around their morning fires, as their day was beginning, and most seemed not to notice the crazed horseman walking past them. He nodded to a few of them and they nodded back, with caution. No one trusted anyone. He must find the soldiers.

He saw Traintors colors flying high above the largest tent and knew the soldiers would be surrounding it. Taking a deep breath and hanging his head down, he proceeded in that direction.

When news reached King Traintor's entourage of what was happening in Welexia, no one wanted to be the one to tell him. They knew he would explode and a torrent of expletives and vile would spill down upon anyone within earshot. Either that, or he would be silent, as he fumed and devised an evil plan. The army commander took it upon himself to address the king.

Bowing down he said, "Your Majesty, I have some distressing news to relay to you."

He was met with a giant putrid burp as the King snapped his fingers for more food.

The commander waited.

Speaking with a mouthful of food he said, "Well, what is it? Has one of my beauties gotten ugly overnight?"

Everyone knew the King kept women captive, using and abusing them. When one of them died because of his brutality, he would say they had gotten ugly. Or he would tell his nearest counsel that he found a particular woman ugly now, which meant he wanted them to disappear. To die. Once in a while they would take their own lives because it was preferable over their living hell.

"No, your Majesty. I mean, not that I know of."

"I'm bored with this conversation. Either reveal this distressing news or get out of my sight." Shifting slightly on his traveling throne he farted. "Haven't we got to pack up and get on the road so another village can fawn over me?"

Much to his chagrin, the commander blurted out, "There has been a revolt at the castle. King Oshinor has been set free."

One of the courtiers gasped and dropped a tray. Speaking the name Oshinor was a sure way to be executed. The silence that followed was crackling with electricity.

Speaking just above a whisper Traintor said, "What did you say?"

The commander's self preservation kicked in. "Your Majesty, the details are hazy. Perhaps I should bring in the guard who has brought the news as he was there to witness it."

Traintor said nothing but motioned with his hand and nodded in the affirmative. Anyone who knew him could tell that he was seething.

The guard was stiff and had trouble walking, after several days astride a horse. He was led in by two soldiers, as though he was a prisoner and not a messenger showing his loyalty. He had never been this close to the king and he shook with fear. All eyes, including Traintor's, were upon him. He was shoved forward and fell hard upon his knees. Holding his head down and looking at the rug beneath him he said, "It is true, My King. Villagers, so many villagers came in the night, two… no… three nights ago, and began releasing all prisoners inside the castle. They were telling people to join them, promising no harm would come to them if they sided with… if they sided with…" He froze. Terror overtook him.

Traintor, sounding calm, yet menacing, said, "Go on. Sided with whom? Just say what it is you believe has happened."

All around him, people were stepping away. Those who had spent any time with this king knew what was coming next. There was always a calm demeanor just before an explosion. They wished to be as far away from the target, in this case, the poor messenger, as they could. A few of them took the opportunity to completely slip out of the tent, intending to pack up and leave as soon as they could. Like the guard, they too had believed Oshinor was dead or far away in a distant land. Until now, they had no idea he was alive.

Traintor stood up and shouted, spittle and bits of food flying from his mouth, "You are lying! Take this man away. How dare you come into my tent to spread such untruths. We all know the cretan king fled in the night, which is why I stepped in to look after all of Welexia. Get him out of my sight. I expect to see him strung up high when we leave this village. Spare no pain with his suffering!"

"But it is true. I only came here to tell you. I have been a loyal subject. Please, no, no!" His words faded as he was dragged out of the tent to the far edge of the encampment where he would succumb to brutality, much like the brutality he had meted out himself, on behalf of this cruel dictator.

Please use the resources below if you need any support.

RAINN (Rape, Abuse, Incest National Network)
Hotline: 1-800-656-HOPE (4673)
National Suicide Prevention Lifeline: 1-800-723-8255

ABOUT THE AUTHOR

Rhys Shaw lives in California with their menagerie of pets, books, and a spouse. Not necessarily in that order. A writer of short stories and poetry, this is their first fiction novel. It is the first in The Welexia Series.

If you enjoyed this book, please leave a review on Amazon. Reviews are important for new authors and I would be eternally grateful for yours - Rhys
https://www.amazon.com/dp/B0B1J8NQGJ?ref_=pe_3052080_276849420

You can also follow Rhys on Facebook
https://www.facebook.com/authorrhysshaw
And Instagram @rhysshawauthor

For more Welexian insights and future book info, please sign up for my newsletter at
https://www.subscribepage.com/rhysshawauthor

Made in the USA
Columbia, SC
02 July 2022